THE BRIDE TO BE

DANIEL HURST

INKUBATOR
BOOKS

Published by Inkubator Books
www.inkubatorbooks.com

Copyright © 2023 by Daniel Hurst

ISBN (eBook): 978-1-83756-161-2
ISBN (Paperback): 978-1-83756-162-9
ISBN (Hardback): 978-1-83756-163-6

Daniel Hurst has asserted his right to be identified as the author of this work.

THE BRIDE TO BE is a work of fiction. People, places, events, and situations are the product of the author's imagination. Any resemblance to actual persons, living or dead is entirely coincidental.

PROLOGUE

A bride is not supposed to get arrested on her wedding day.

The fact that such a shocking and strange thing was happening was the reason dozens of guests were standing around outside the exclusive country manor on this sprawling estate, gawking and gossiping as they watched the unusual scene unfold.

The dazzling white of the woman's wedding dress was in stark contrast to the dark uniforms of the police officers who were leading the bride to one of the vehicles, their flashing blue lights reflecting off the glass windows of the impressive building behind them.

The glint of the metallic handcuffs wrapped around the suspect's wrists was almost as bright as all the pink confetti that lay untouched in the baskets held by the bridesmaids, four women who could not believe that their best friend was being taken into custody on what should have been the happiest day of her life.

The bride herself was angry and frustrated, as well she

might be, ignoring the warning she had been issued a moment ago in that anything she said may be used as evidence against her at a later date. But while she was speaking freely, her movements were much more restricted, and that was because of the two burly officers holding an arm each and escorting her into the car, pushing her head down and bundling her into the backseat before slamming the door shut and leaving her trapped on the other side of the glass from all her invited guests.

It was as she stared out through the window of the police car that she saw the tall man in the dark suit standing at the top of the steps in front of the entrance to the manor. He was looking right back at her, his dark brown eyes boring into her soul. They were eyes that she thought she would get to look into for many years to come once this wedding day had gone as planned. Through the honeymoon, through the first few years of marriage, in the hospital when they had their first child together and even at the end, as one of them lay on their death bed and prepared to say goodbye. But as the officer behind the wheel started the engine and began to navigate away from the congregation of well-dressed attendees, the bride in the handcuffs saw one more thing.

She saw the woman who might have been to blame for all of this.

A woman who had not heeded her warning to stay away...

BEFORE THE WEDDING

1

Rather predictably, the station is busy as I make my way towards the ticket barriers alongside the dozens of other people who are out and about on this warm Saturday morning. Perhaps it's the increase in temperature that has seen so many people dare to venture into London today, and as I squeeze through the barriers, I'm nudged and bumped by all sorts of naked limbs belonging to fellow travellers in shorts or crop tops or short-sleeved shirts.

Yes, there's no doubt about it. If everyone is starting to wear fewer clothes, then it can only mean one thing.

Summer is here.

Or rather, wedding season is here.

That realisation causes my stomach to churn as I make my way onto the platform and glance up at the screen to see that the next train is due in two minutes' time. Wedding season is most definitely upon us, and this year, I will be one of the hundreds of people who will be playing a very active role in that scene. No longer will I be a passive observer or a participant with a very small role in a wedding. I'm not going to be a guest or a bridesmaid who can just turn up, smile for the cameras and savour a few glasses of champagne while watching the happy couple go through the real endeavours of the day. No, the next wedding I attend calls for me to be front and centre, in the limelight, the star of the show.

I'm getting married in one month's time.

Finally, I am going to be the one in the white dress.

So why the nerves as I see the train approaching over the tops of the heads of all the other passengers waiting to get on board? Why am I not overwhelmed with excitement about marrying the man I love in front of all my family and friends? Am I feeling sick because I'm nervous about making the walk down the aisle, or cutting the cake, or getting my vows wrong?

No, I'm nervous because of one very important thing, and as the train comes to a stop and the nearest doors slide open in front of me, I think about that thing once again.

I still haven't found my wedding dress.

I catch sight of my reflection in the train windows as I step towards the door, and while I'm currently make-up free and sporting a hairstyle that can best be described as unkempt, I know I'll be making far more of an effort on my big day. My dark hair will be styled, and my face will have been worked on by a professional make-up artist, a woman who will do all she can to accentuate my brown eyes and high cheekbones. While I might be thirty-eight, I have been assured that the artist works wonders and will have me looking ten years younger after she's finished with me. I hope she is a woman of her word, because while I'm not old and haggard by any stretch of the imagination, who doesn't want to appear younger if they can?

I'm sweating as I step onto the train, but it only has a

little to do with the heat inside the carriage and a lot more to do with the fact that I'm aware time is running out for me to find my perfect dress. To put it bluntly, today might be one of my last chances to get the dress side of things sorted, and that is why, as the carriage fills up and I cling onto the handrail beside me, I have to hope that my appointment this morning goes well.

I am on my way to the wedding shop on Church Lane, an apt address for such a business, and I am going there to try on as many dresses as I can. My appointment is at midday, and as the train lurches forward and begins to leave the station, a quick check on my watch tells me that I should be able to make it just in time. I lost a few minutes as I was leaving the house when my fiancé, Mark, kept talking to me, wanting to know what time I would be back even though I'd already told him, but as long as this train encounters no delays, then I'll be fine.

Estimating that I've got about fifteen minutes before I reach my stop, I reach into my handbag and pull out my headphones before jamming them in my ears and going in search of my favourite podcast. Desperate to drown out the noises from my fellow passengers, but just as desperate to listen to what has become my go-to show for all things weddings, I quickly find the next episode of the podcast and press play. When I do, I hear the familiar theme tune begin, a theme tune I must have heard over a hundred times since a colleague at work told me that if I was getting married, then I should listen to the *Marriage Mayhem* podcast. I'm glad I took her advice because no sooner had I listened to the first episode than I realised I wasn't the first person in the world to be panicking about their upcoming nuptials. I also realised that it would go on to be an invaluable source of tips and tricks to help me navigate the sometimes confusing, stressful and often downright debilitating process of trying to plan a wedding.

'Are you getting married? Are you feeling overwhelmed? Fear not, because the Marriage Mayhem podcast is here for you. With professional wedding planner Susie Burrows and first-time bride-to-be Amy Gallagher, we will guide you through every step of your journey, turning the "I don't know what I'm doing" into the "I do".'

I take a deep breath as I listen to the familiar opening segment of the podcast, feeling a little calmer now that I'm in the presence of old friends. Okay, so I might not have actually met Susie or Amy in person, but that doesn't mean I don't know them. I've listened to them talking for countless hours over the last ten months, ever since the day my fiancé got down on one knee and popped the question, and that means I feel part of them now. They are kind and informative and witty, and thanks to this podcast, I have been able to tick many things off my very full wedding to-do list.

Susie gave me a great idea for organising the table plan, while Amy gave a wonderful breakdown of the pros and cons of using a videographer to record the day instead of a photographer. I wouldn't have known to ask certain questions about the wedding venue if it weren't for these two presenters giving their listeners a rundown of the really important things to find out before making a booking. And, for sure, I wouldn't have known the best way of dealing with all the late-night anxiety that often threatens to overwhelm an anxious bride as the day of the nuptials draws nearer.

As Susie and Amy open another show by thanking a few of their listeners for some generous donations lately to help with their running costs, I remind myself that I'm not the first woman in the world to struggle to find a wedding dress, and I won't be the last. But thanks to episode 16 of this podcast, an episode I have listened to three times in total now, I know that the key is not to panic and, most importantly, not rush into getting any old dress just to get it done. I am entitled to want to take my time and try on multiple dresses, and while I obviously can't take forever to make my mind up, this is my big day, and I should feel happy with whatever I choose to wear as I walk down the aisle.

I'm just about managing to lose myself in the words coming out of my headphones enough to temporarily forget that I'm on a crowded train in the stifling heat, but I'm snapped back into the moment when several messages start arriving on my phone. Checking my notifications, I see that my best friend and chief bridesmaid, Molly, is eagerly messaging me and the rest of our friends in my wedding WhatsApp group, and it's no surprise to learn what has got her so excited.

Seven days to go until the hen party, girls!

This time next week, we'll be dancing on tables in Manchester!

Oh Kate, we have so much planned for you! You better be worried!

I can't help but smile as I see several of my other friends reply, saying they are all just as excited as Molly, and I make sure to reply too.

I can't wait. But please go gentle on me...

I have no doubt that they will not bear that in mind next Saturday and dread to think what might be waiting for me. Gyrating male strippers with oiled-up abs? Probably, but if that's all, then I can count myself lucky.

I'm sure Molly could do much worse, and for all I know, she intends to.

While I'm a part of this particular WhatsApp group, I am forbidden from the official Hen Party group in which the actual plans for my last weekend of freedom with my best mates are discussed. Therefore, I have no idea what might be waiting for me this time next week beyond us going to Manchester, and I can't help but feel a little envious of Mark, who has already had his stag do and, therefore, no longer has to worry what pranks his friends might play on him. He went to Portugal for a weekend of male debauchery, and he came back smiling but utterly exhausted, so tired that he required two days off work the following week just to recover. I envision feeling the same when I get home, and as Molly messages me privately to tell me that she loves me and is super determined to give me the best weekend of my life, I thank her and know whatever is in store, she only has my interests at heart.

We've been best friends since our school days, and while she might like to try to lead me astray from time to time, she's always looked out for me, which is why I made her my chief bridesmaid. She's been a pillar of support during this time, saving me from many a meltdown when I've become overwhelmed with wedding planning, and I'll never forget that. So while I may very well have some chiselled guy flapping his private parts near my face next weekend, that's a problem for another day, and as the messages briefly die down again, I go back to paying attention to the podcast.

The hosts are currently discussing the age-old wedding dilemma of whether to get a band or a DJ for the evening entertainment portion of the big day, and I listen to both sides of the debate as the train rumbles on. By the time it comes to a stop at my station, the hosts have agreed that either a DJ or a band will work as long as they are kept on a tight leash and given a strict setlist of songs to stick to, and I smile because that is one job I can confidently say I have already ticked off. I sent the list of my and Mark's favourite songs to the DJ we have booked, and that is one less thing to worry about as the train doors open and I squeeze myself through the densely packed passengers blocking my escape route.

As I disembark and hurry along the platform towards the exit, I cross my fingers and hope that today is the day I lay my eyes on my dream wedding dress.

Little did I know it then, but it would be.

However, it would also be the day I laid eyes on something else I wanted.

Something forbidden.

2

The glass of champagne that I was offered shortly after entering the shop is on the table beside the sofa where I am currently sitting while anxiously awaiting the arrival of the dress I asked the assistant to bring me. Her name is Chrissy, and she looks a little younger than me, although she tells me she already has a decade's worth of experience in helping brides-to-be choose their dresses, so I guess she knows what she's doing. I certainly hope so as I see her re-emerge from the back of the shop holding the hook upon which hangs the next dress I am going to try on.

'This will be the closest one in your size,' Chrissy tells me with a smile. 'Let's try it on and see what you think, and of course, we can have it altered if you do decide to go with it.'

'Thank you,' I say as I make my way towards the changing rooms, silently praying that this dress will look as good on me as it looks hanging on the rack.

After welcoming me into the shop half an hour ago, Chrissy talked me through the array of dresses on display in this large store, and having done so, I have selected this particular one to try on first. But overall, I think this must be at least the twelfth dress I have tried on over the last few months, so I'm not getting my hopes up too much. There's always been something wrong with the previous ones, whether they have made my arms look fat or revealed too much of my cleavage or not enough of my back or vice versa.

It's hard enough finding a nice sweatshirt or pair of jeans to wear, but finding the dress that will be photographed a gazillion times by everybody who knows you?

Yeah, that's a little tougher.

Pulling the curtain closed so that I have a little privacy in this small changing room, I begin to undress, trying not to glance at my semi-naked body too much as my clothes come off because, despite promising myself that I'd lose some weight before my big day, I've not lost quite as much as I'd hoped. But who has time to go to the gym when there's invites to send out, floral arrangements to be made and emails from the wedding venue to reply to?

Chrissy discreetly joins me in the changing room and carefully helps me into the dress, but like she warned me, we both know it's not the exact size I require. I'm trying not to let that put me off, because that can be worked on, so I smooth out any creases in the white fabric that clings to my body before looking in the mirror.

When I do, I let out a sigh.

This dress is nice.

But it's still not the one.

I might only have been wearing it for less than a minute, but the consensus from people who have been through this before me was that I would know it the second I saw the perfect dress. If I'm unsure, then it's not right, and I already know this is not quite it.

'It's not really me, is it?' I tell Chrissy, and she helps me back out of it and leaves me to get dressed again.

Once again I'm down to my underwear. It's then that I hear the bell ring above the front door to the shop. That's followed by Chrissy welcoming somebody into the shop before offering them a glass of champagne, and I hear another female voice say, 'Thanks but no thanks.'

'Damn it,' I mutter to myself as I start dressing again, and by the time I've got the jeans back on, I am reminding myself to keep calm. It took Molly a while to find her perfect dress, just like it took most of my friends several attempts before they landed on what they wanted. And according to Susan and Amy on the podcast, they struggled too, so I'm far from alone in this.

But while that's comforting, something else isn't.

I can't take forever to make my mind up.

Back in my scruffy clothing, I leave the dressing room with the beautiful but not-quite-right dress on its hanger. Chrissy smiles; she doesn't look too disappointed at our lack of luck because she has plenty more garments for me to try yet. But she does look a little tired, and as she sips from her coffee cup, I notice that there is no wedding ring on her finger.

I wonder if it's odd that a woman who spends all day surrounded by the idea of marriage hasn't actually entered into it herself yet, but I don't want to pry. Like me and my seemingly endless search for the right dress, maybe she has just never been able to find the right man or woman to spend the rest of her life with. That's a shame if she is looking, because everyone deserves a little slice of happiness, but maybe she has no interest in settling down anytime soon. Perhaps being around stressed-out women worrying over their own weddings has put her off the idea of inflicting that anguish on herself, and who could blame her if so? Sometimes, rarely but on occasion, I do look back on my single days and think about how simple life was then. It was a lot of fun, but being single only stays fun if you have other single friends to enjoy it with. The enjoyment sure did start to dry up when all my pals started coupling up, tying the knot and having babies, and before I knew it, I couldn't find anybody to go out with on a Friday night.

But then I met Mark, and the rest, as they say, is history.

Browsing yet another selection of dresses, I tell myself that my fortunes are soon about to change, and I'm only a matter of minutes away from finding what I'm looking for. But as I do that, I hear the voice I heard earlier. It's the woman who entered the shop while I was in the changing room, and as I glance towards the other end of the shop, I see a flash of blonde hair poking out from behind a mannequin wearing a sequinned white ballgown.

The woman is talking to somebody, though I'm not sure who because I can't see anyone with her, and Chrissy is still near me over on this side, but I keep looking, and when I see her step out fully from behind the mannequin, I can't help but gasp.

She is gorgeous.

I am a certified heterosexual, but I will always happily admit when I'm in the presence of a beautiful female, and I'm certainly in the presence of one now. Tall, slender and toned, this woman looks like a goddess as she moves amongst the wedding dresses on display, so much so that I can scarcely comprehend how stunning she will look when she's wearing one of them. Envy is not a good thing, but I find myself wishing I were as slim as her, not to mention as tall, and I certainly wouldn't say no to those eyelashes either. This woman could walk down the aisle in a bin bag, and I bet she'd still look elegant. But the same can't be said for me because I'm going to require a small army of professionals to get me all beautified before my big moment.

'This is nice, don't you think, darling?'

She speaks again, but I still don't see whom she is talking to, or at least I don't until I hear a chair creak before somebody steps out from behind the wall that's partially blocking my view. When they do, I see a dark, handsome man wearing a sharp suit, and if I was in awe of the woman, I can only say that I am blown away by him.

He looks like a movie star, the kind who get paid millions because their face alone can sell cinema tickets and see posters spring up all over town. Devilishly handsome, well-groomed but looking more vulnerable than arrogant, there's no doubt that this guy must have been a real heartbreaker in his single days. But I guess those are long gone now, because he is standing beside the beautiful blonde and examining the dress alongside her. However, the more I look, the more I feel like there is something vaguely familiar about this man, although I can't quite figure out what it might be.

'Caught you staring.'

I almost jump out of my skin when I hear Chrissy's voice behind me, and as I turn around, I do my best to pretend like I wasn't just gawking at the picture-perfect couple in the shop. But it's no good because Chrissy has clearly rumbled me.

'It's okay, I get it. They look like A-listers,' she says with a chuckle. 'Although despite asking their names and doing a quick internet search, they are not movie stars as far as I can tell. How about another glass of champagne?'

'No, I'm fine, thanks,' I say, not wanting to have the bubbles go to my head and make my search for a dress even trickier than it already is.

Chrissy nods and goes to wander off, very much looking like she wishes she could have a strong drink of her own, but before she can get out of earshot, I quietly ask her a question.

'Isn't it bad luck for the groom to see the bride's dress before the big day?' I say, referring to the couple, who seem to be shopping together.

'Yes, usually it is,' Chrissy replies. 'But they aren't following traditions, apparently.'

'Oh, I see.'

I wait until Chrissy has wandered off again before I look back at the couple and watch them some more, and as I do, I see the woman clearly has no qualms about her partner being here with her today. I can't imagine inviting Mark to be with me as I shop for a dress and not just because I feel like the moment a bride reveals herself should be a surprise for the groom. It's because shopping with him would be a nightmare, no matter what we were looking for. He'd be moaning and groaning and checking his phone and just doing anything but paying attention to the job at hand, as he often does whenever we go to the supermarket together or onto the high street. He hates shopping, so he'd surely make this even more of a trying experience if he were here. But that woman seems to be having no such problems with her partner; he is following behind her closely and offering his opinion when it is asked of him. He is even suggesting a few things of his own, showing just how engaged he is with the whole process.

Who is this man?

And who is the woman who has snared him?

Those are questions that stay on my mind as I continue to shop, and while I don't see the couple look over at me at any point, I make sure to keep checking on them and listening to whatever it is they might be talking about. That's how I hear when the woman says she thinks she might have just found the perfect dress, and it's also how I hear when the man says he thinks it is perfect too.

It seems they have found what they are looking for. As they make their way over to Chrissy, who is sitting behind a desk, staring abjectly out of the window at the pedestrians passing by, they seem to be ready to let her know that they wish to place their order.

I'm jealous of them, though not just because their search for a dress appears to be at an end while mine goes on.

I'm jealous of them because they seem genuinely happy and excited about their upcoming wedding.

But I can't say the same thing.

3

As I step outside the shop and squint in the bright sunlight, I know I should be feeling disappointed about not finding a dress. But I'm not, because there is something else occupying my mind – and that is making sure I don't lose sight of the couple who are walking away down the street ahead of me.

Setting off quickly so that too big a distance can't develop between us, I follow the couple as they make their way down the busy street, hand in hand and chatting away to each other. Even if they were to glance back, they might not notice me because there are plenty of other pedestrians I'm walking alongside. But I don't want to take the chance of them thinking I'm stalking them, so I slow my pace a little and increase the distance between us slightly.

But I am not stalking them.

Absolutely not.

If I had to put a label on what I'm currently doing, then I would say that I am being curious. But it's not just because I have this strange feeling that I might know this man from somewhere. Like me, these people are about to get married, so we have that in common, as well as the fact we were both in the dress shop at the same time. I'm curious as to where they might be going next, possibly looking to tick off another item on their to-do list. After finding the right dress for her, are they now on their way to find the right suit for him? Might they be going to window-shop for a necklace for her, one that will complement her wedding-day attire and be easier to buy now they have a better idea about the neckline of the dress? Or are they going to a travel agency to go over a few more details about the exotic honeymoon they have planned for after the nuptials are complete? It's hard to guess, not least because Chrissy told me that this couple were not going to do things the traditional way, and that intrigues me enough to want to find out a lot more about them.

Oh, who am I kidding? I am attracted to the handsome man and fascinated by his pretty partner, a woman who does not seem overwhelmed by this whole wedding malarky at all, and that is really the only reason I am trailing them now instead of going to the train station and travelling home like I should.

I track them around the corner and onto another street, but besides briefly pausing by the window of a shop and spending a minute or so looking inside, they have otherwise remained on the move. I'm beginning to wonder just how far they might be walking, well aware that every step I take leads me farther away from the station I should really be at by now. But when I see them cross the road and walk up to the front door of a gastropub called the Carter Arms, a building tucked away down a quiet street off the main road, I see they have finally arrived at their next destination.

The man holds the door open for his partner so she can enter the pub first, a gentlemanly act that only increases his value in my eyes. But then the door closes, and they are out of sight, leaving me alone on the street, staring at the pub and wondering what to do next.

Okay, this is enough. Now it's time to go home. I've already delayed too much, and if I'm not careful, Mark will start to wonder what is taking me so long. He'll be at the gym now for his weekly HIIT class, but that finishes at four, and I told him I'd be back by then. I can still make it if I leave now, but it'll be touch and go if I dither out here any longer.

So why am I now walking towards the pub?

I open the door and tell myself that I will just have one quick drink, and then I really will go home, but while I do, I might as well have another quick look at that couple and see if I learn anything more about them. But where are they? The pub is packed, many drinkers here seemingly out to watch the England cricket match that is showing on the various television screens hanging on the wall around the venue. But beyond the heads of the mostly male crowd in here, I see a few tables, and it's there where I spot the woman again. She's sitting at a table and reading the food menu. But where is her partner? It only takes a few seconds for me to locate him too. He's standing at the bar and placing his drinks order with the young woman behind it, and as she gets to work, pouring a pint for him and making a gin and tonic for her, I take my place at the opposite end of the bar.

'What will it be, love?' a barman asks me, surprising me as he pops up from below the bar, where he must have been restocking a glasses shelf or perhaps cleaning something during a brief lull in serving customers.

'Erm, I'll just have a lemonade, thanks,' I say, and I note

the disappointment on his face because I haven't given him anything more challenging to make, or maybe it's just because this place really could do with earning some more money, and a soft drink is hardly going to make much of a difference to the finances.

But he gets on with pouring me my drink, and once he has, I take my glass and find myself a small table in the corner, one that offers me a poor view of the cricket on the TV but an excellent view of the couple across the pub.

They are saying very little to each other, but that's only because they are both distracted with the menu, and while they make their choices for dinner, I think about the last time I went out for a meal with my partner. It was a while ago now. We went to a Greek restaurant, but only after I suggested we get out of the house instead of spending another Saturday night on the sofa. We used to do all sorts of fun things together when we first started dating, but I suppose you could say that things have been less exciting lately, although Mark did remind me that with a wedding to save for, we should tighten the purse strings a little. I suppose that is sensible, but after managing to get him to join me at the Greek restaurant, I had hoped for a nice evening of good conversation over generous portions of pitta breads, tzatziki and gyros. Unfortunately, it didn't quite go to plan, although I was slightly to blame for that.

I accidentally knocked my glass of red wine over Mark just before our main courses could be served, staining his cream chinos and ruining the relaxed mood somewhat. He was initially annoyed but calmed down when the waiter came to offer his assistance, dabbing at Mark's trousers with a napkin, although that only seemed to stain the napkin almost as much as the trousers. In the end, Mark told him to leave it, and we waited for our food, but no sooner had it come than Mark just wanted to eat quickly and go home.

I suppose it can't have been much fun to sit in a busy restaurant in wet chinos, knowing that everybody else in there saw the incident with the wine and possibly had a little giggle over it. But it was a shame that it ruined what would have probably been a nice evening for the two of us, and since then, I've not been too keen to suggest we go out for another meal. The wedding is drawing closer now, so I could do with avoiding those extra calories, though I admit to being a little envious when I see the man go back to the bar again and place his order. I can't hear what he's asking for, but I imagine it's something a little naughty for the waistline, like pub food often is. A burger perhaps or maybe a steak. My stomach rumbles at the thought of a bowl of chips or a salad drenched in dressing, but I make do with my lemonade and watch as the man pays and returns to his table, holding a number so he can be easily found when his food is ready.

He chats to his fiancée as they wait for their meal to arrive, and when I see her reach out to take his hand across the table, he is as quick to take hers too, an affectionate gesture in amongst all the chunnering and chattering men grumbling about the state of the English batsmen.

They look so happy. So in love. So right for each other.

I know nothing about them other than that they are getting married soon, but I want what they have.

I want to be happy.

I also know what I don't want as I sit here and make this drink last as long as I possibly can.

I don't want to go home and see my fiancé.

4

After getting off the train and making the short walk from the station to the street on which I live, I approach my property with a sense of trepidation. Is Mark's car going to be on the driveway, or am I going to have beaten him home? But the fact that my watch tells me that it is almost five o'clock means I feel like I already know the answer.

I'm late.

And sure enough, Mark is back before me.

I take my phone out of my handbag and check it for messages, but, unsurprisingly, there are none. Mark has not bothered to contact me to check where I am or even just express his frustration that I am out later than I said I would be. But of course he hasn't.

He would never do that.

He vents his frustration in far more subtle ways.

But I'm emboldened by the albeit slim chance that he might not be annoyed at me and actually have no issue with me being late. There's just as much chance of him being perfectly fine with me and asking me how my afternoon was as there is of him being grumpy. That's the thing with Mark. I never quite know what mood he will be in, which can be disconcerting, but I guess we're all different, and none of us can profess to being in the same state of mind every single day, can we?

As I walk past Mark's car and take out my front door key, I wonder if this will be one of the times when I arrive home to find him cooking for me, the table already set and a bottle of wine opened while music plays on the radio and the overall atmosphere in the house is a positive one. I sure do hope so, and not just because I'm hungry. It's because today, after journeying back and forth into London and ultimately leaving the wedding dress shop empty-handed, I feel like I need it to be an easy homecoming.

But there's another reason I'm silently praying for it to all go well as I slide my key into the lock and twist it. After watching that happy couple for the last couple of hours, I very much wish to have a slice of my own happiness and have what they have, for a short while at least. But that remains to be seen, and as I step into the house, I wonder what I'll get.

Happy Mark.

Or moody Mark.

The fact that my nostrils don't detect any hint of a meal being cooked is not a good first sign, but maybe Mark has decided we could order a takeaway tonight, so I won't read too much into things yet. But there's no music playing either, which would have been a hint that my fiancé was enjoying his Saturday and not caring too much about what might have held me up in London. And then I get confirmation of exactly how Mark is feeling as the door to the living room swings open, and no sooner has he seen me taking off my coat than the questions start.

'What time do you call this? Where the hell have you been?'

Oh no. This is not going to be a fun night.

Forcing a smile onto my face to cover my disappointment, I hang my coat on the hook at the foot of the stairs before stepping towards my fiancé and opening up my arms as if to give him a hug.

'Sorry, love. I was longer than I thought I would be at the shop, and then the trains were a little delayed when I was coming back.'

That last part is a white lie, but what else could I say? That I followed a couple to a pub and watched them eating a meal while I sat alone and wondered why my partner didn't take me out more often?

'You said you'd be home when I got back from the gym. This isn't good enough.'

Mark steps away from me so I can't give him the hug I wanted to before he disappears back into the living room, and when I follow him in, I find him sitting on the sofa with the remote control in his hand. He turns the TV on then, and from the way it looks, it's as if he has nothing more to say to me.

'Aren't you going to ask me how it went at the shop?' I ask him, wishing he were showing more of an interest in the wedding and what I might be planning on wearing for it.

'What's the point? I already know the answer,' he grumbles back, his eyes never leaving the TV as he speaks. 'Let me guess. You didn't find the right dress.'

He glances at me, and my face gives away the answer

without me having to speak, and that seems to be funny because he starts laughing then. But it's not the kind of laughter that one would produce after hearing a funny joke. It's more of a sarcastic laughter, as if he is not really laughing with me but *at me*.

'Brilliant. I'm getting married in four weeks, and my fiancée hasn't even found a dress yet. That's not a problem at all, is it?'

Mark shakes his head before turning back to the TV, so dismissive, as if I'm letting him down on purpose.

'Don't be like that. I tried six dresses on and looked at a dozen more. I really want to find one. I'm just struggling, that's all. But there's still time.'

'Just pick one! Any dress will do, I don't care!'

'But I do! I want it to be perfect, just like I want everything about the day to be perfect!'

'But nothing's perfect, is it? I'll be glad when the whole thing is over with, and we're married. If I'd had any idea how much hassle this whole thing was, then I wouldn't have bothered.'

'Mark, don't say that!'

Tears well up in my eyes, but I quickly wipe them away before Mark can see, not that there's much danger of that because his eyes are glued to the TV.

'I promise I'll find a dress soon. I'm getting closer.'

'Whatever.'

Mark turns the volume up then so that the newsreader's voice drowns out whatever I might want to say next.

I go to leave the living room, but before I do, Mark calls out to ask me what time I'm making dinner for, and while I feel like snapping back and telling him to cook something himself, I bite my lip and leave it.

Don't make his mood worse, I silently say to myself. *I am late, so it's my fault he's mad at me.*

I tell Mark that I'll have our evening meal ready in about half an hour before going into the kitchen and making a start on it. But while my hands are busy grabbing food items from the fridge and placing pans down on top of the stove, my mind is running riot as I think about the situation I'm in and how my life has come to this.

Despite sometimes being a lovely, pleasant man, Mark is just as equally a rude, offensive and uncaring bore who doesn't hesitate to say something that might upset me when- ever he feels like it. But that's all he does. He says words that are designed to hurt me. He doesn't text them to me or leave them on a voicemail because doing such a thing runs the risk of me having evidence that I might show to another person and blow up the façade he has created of being a loving partner. Nor has he ever got physically violent with me, a fact I am grateful for, although it's saying a lot when I have to consider myself fortunate that my fiancé hasn't hit me yet. But as far as living with Mark on a daily basis goes, it's occasionally unpleasant and quite often downright disturbing.

So why don't I just leave him?

I know for a fact that if I were ten years younger, then I wouldn't hesitate to walk out the front door and never look back. Maybe I'd still do it if I were five years younger. But I'm thirty-eight and fast approaching thirty-nine, and that's the reason I stay.

I want to be a wife. I want to have a family. I want what all my friends have got.

But I feel like time will run out for me if I go back to square one now.

As I chop an onion while a portion of red mince slowly starts to brown in the hot pan beside me, I think about how I met Mark and how, when I did, I thought I had been salvaged from the scrapheap of life. It was two years ago, and the chance encounter came at a time when I was doing a lot of soul-searching about my personal life. Having lost count of how many times I'd been a bridesmaid, or how many times I'd been to a hen party, or how many times I'd gushed over photos of somebody else's baby, I was wondering if I was ever going to have my own wedding and my own child. But having been single for a while, and with my love life practically non-existent thanks to a string of bad dates or late nights working when I could have been out mingling, I had started to give up hope.

Enter Mark, the attractive man who was next to me at the self-service checkouts in a 24/7 supermarket late one night as I was making my way home from yet another disastrous date. I'd called into the supermarket to pick up a bottle of wine, which I planned to drown my sorrows with as soon as I got back to my flat. But before I could make the purchase and be on my way, I heard the groaning from the man next to me.

'Damn it. Why don't they take cards? Who has cash on them these days?'

I looked up to see a handsome but somewhat-stressed guy trying to buy his own bottle of wine but struggling to complete the transaction, mainly because he only had a bank card on him, while the checkout he was at only allowed for payment by cash.

I considered just keeping myself to myself, but I was also feeling like I should try to be a good Samaritan if only because it might result in some positive karma coming my

way one day in the future. And so I offered Mark the spare
ten-pound note I had in my purse.

He'd been surprised to see that I was offering to pay for
his purchase, no doubt because we were complete strangers,
and I surely had no way of ever expecting the money to be
returned to me. But I insisted, and once the wine was officially his, he continued to thank me as we made our way out
of the supermarket. I told him not to think anything more of
it, but he did, so much so that we got chatting about our
evening and the reasons why we were out purchasing
alcohol alone so late on a weekday night.

I told him about the date I'd just come from with the guy
who had bored me to tears for two hours with stories about
how much money he was making for his boss in his banking
job, and in return, my new friend told me that he was on his
way home from work after a particularly gruelling day in the
office. Enjoying his company and his attention as we
continued to talk, I tried not to glance at his left hand but
eventually found it impossible to resist, and when I saw that
there was no ring there, I admit to being more than a little
excited. My excitement only grew when he asked me if I
would care to endure one more date that week, and this
time, it would be with him.

*I said yes, the date was arranged, and that was how I met
Mark.*

Dropping the onion into the pan and the knife I cut it
with into the dishwasher, I stir the mince to make sure all of
it is cooked. But while this meal will be ready soon, I can't
say I'm looking forward to sitting down and eating it with
Mark. Maybe if he was like how he was when we went on
our first date, then it would be fine. But he's not. He waited
until I was in love with him and had bought a house with

him before he started to slowly reveal the other side to his personality. But it was only when I had accepted his marriage proposal that he really revealed it, most likely because he knew then that I would be too embarrassed to call the whole thing off, having already told my friends.

He knows I feared growing old alone, with no partner, no children to raise and having a different life to all my friends, and he exploited that, treating me well on occasion but badly on others, and, all the while, confident that I wouldn't leave him.

And he's been right so far.

I haven't left him.

And because of that, as our wedding day continues to draw nearer, I can't help but feel even worse about the whole thing.

5

Despite having my tastebuds tickled earlier when I sat in the pub and watched that couple eat their meal, I have to admit that my own dinner this evening was a complete disaster.

Feeling down about Mark's attitude towards me when I came home, mixed with my ever-increasing anxiety about my inability to find the right wedding dress, led to me burning the food to the point where it was barely edible. Things got so bad that I even managed to set the smoke alarm off at one point, forcing me to go running out into the hallway and wave a tea towel above my head to disperse the smoke. That obviously drew Mark's attention, and with the smell of burning food in his nostrils, he entered the kitchen to see the charred remains of the meal I had attempted to make.

It was at that point that I expected him to admonish and criticise me for ruining dinner, because he was already mad at me, so it wouldn't take much to irritate him some more. But that was when Mark once again displayed his trademark style of always keeping me guessing, and rather than critique my efforts, he told me not to worry about it.

'I'll go and get us takeaway pizzas,' he told me before he scraped the burnt food into the bin. Then, after giving me a kiss on the forehead as he passed me, he put on his coat and left the house. That was ten minutes ago, and of course, I've spent every single one of those ten minutes wondering what kind of mood Mark will be in when he gets back.

This unpredictable behaviour drives me mad, and I wish I could see some kind of pattern in it so I could perhaps find a way of ensuring there were more good moods than bad. But I've never been able to do that, and I wonder if that is by Mark's design, him being well aware that if he doesn't fall into a routine, then I can never truly be at ease in our relationship.

Not for the first time since my fiancé's behaviour gave me cause for concern, I consider rushing upstairs and packing my things and then leaving the house before Mark can get home. I've often entertained the idea of turning up on Molly's doorstep, confident that my best friend would take me in for as long as I needed to get my life back in order. Sure, it would take some explaining on my part, and no doubt plenty of tears would be shed, but I know I would have her full support in whatever I chose to do. I also have the option of going to my parents' house, although they live a couple of hours away, not that they wouldn't come to pick me up if I asked them. Failing that, I could just go to a hotel and check in for a few nights, giving myself some space and providing Mark with a little time to think about his actions and how he might be better off changing them if he wants me to stick around.

In fact, I actually tried the hotel tactic once before, three months ago now, after yet another example of Mark taking out his bad mood on me for no reason.

After a pleasant evening in which the two of us had gone into town to watch the latest Hollywood blockbuster at the cinema, we had come home later than usual and started to get ready for bed. We'd both been chatting away about the film we'd just seen and seemed to be in agreement that it was one of the better movies we'd watched in a while. But then, in the blink of an eye, Mark's demeanour changed towards me, and once again, I was wrong footed and left wondering what the hell I had done to set him off.

Out of nowhere, he accused me of being untidy, citing the few toiletry items of mine that were by the sink, although they had been there for several days, and he hadn't had a problem with them before. Then he told me that I'd been eating my popcorn rather loudly in the cinema, and it had interrupted his enjoyment of the movie a little. They were silly things to say and not particularly hurtful on the face of it, but it was the way he just randomly came out with them, as if he knew I was in a good mood and had to find something to bring me down before we went to sleep. But the final straw came as I was getting into bed and he had a go at me for leaving a light on downstairs. Admittedly, I had been the last person to come upstairs, so it was technically me who had forgot to switch the light off, but it was hardly a crime of epic proportions, and it staggered me that he was treating it as such. That was why I had snapped back at him and told him to calm down, but that only made things worse, and after a heated argument, I decided to take a stand. I had had enough, and to prove it, I got dressed and told him I was going to sleep elsewhere that night.

I hoped that Mark would apologise then and tell me to

stay, but he didn't, so I had little choice but to go through with my threat, and as I left the house, I had no idea where I would go. It was far too late to go to Molly's or any other of my friends', so I ended up at a hotel and booked myself a room for the night. But I didn't sleep much. Instead, I spent the whole night lying awake and thinking of what my life would be like if I was to officially leave Mark. But as I did, I didn't like the vision of my future I saw ahead of me.

Lots of lonely nights, lots of sympathetic stares from my friends and family and, worst of all, the realisation that I was very much back at the beginning of what had already proven to be a long and arduous journey to get me to the point where I could finally become a wife. And that's before I'd even got to the part where I tried to amicably sort out the sale of the house I'd bought with Mark back when things seemed to be much smoother between us.

There is no way that splitting finances would be fun.

All that was why, after checking out of the hotel the following morning, I went back home and apologised to Mark. And guess what he did? He apologised right back before telling me that he loved me and didn't want to lose me, making me feel even more stupid for entertaining the idea of leaving him.

I'm well aware what is going on here. I'm in an abusive relationship, and that abuse is psychological. I have no visible bruising to show anybody, nor can I offer any evidence of any kind. Everything that has gone on between Mark and me has always been behind closed doors, and the crazy thing is that if I was to ask any of my friends what they think of Mark, they would all tell me that he was a wonderful guy and that I'd done well to end up with him. And sometimes, in his better moments, I feel that way too.

And then there are other times, like tonight, as I sit here alone on the sofa and try not to cry as I wait for Mark to come back from the takeaway with the pizzas we only need because I burnt our food.

It's while I'm waiting for him to get back that I receive a text from Molly, and when I read it, I can't hold off the tears any longer.

> I know I've been winding you up on the group chat lately about your hen party, but you know it's only because I love you. I'm so excited to give you the best weekend of your life next weekend, just before you have the best day of your life with Mark next month! So happy for you, bestie! xxx

A teardrop falls onto the screen of my phone, and I wipe it away quickly before grabbing a tissue and dabbing it against my wet eyes. I know that the reason the text triggered me is because it epitomises my problem.

Everybody thinks my life is perfect.

But nobody, not even my best friend, has the slightest clue how I'm really feeling.

No sooner have I stopped crying and blown my nose than I hear the front door open, and when it does, I hear Mark call out to me from the hallway.

'Hey, babe. I'm back! I hope you're hungry because I've got us a feast!'

Mark's cheerful tone is in stark contrast to the way he spoke to me earlier, and as I force myself to go into the kitchen and join him, he opens two large pizza boxes as well as a small side of garlic bread. I know it's happening once again. First he was mad at me and felt I couldn't do anything right, and now he's back to being the loveable fiancé who will do anything for me.

'Tuck in, love. Can I get you a drink?' he asks as he pulls out a chair for me at the table, being super attentive, so much so that he notices I've been crying and looks devastated.

'Oh, come here. What is it?' he asks as he wraps his arms around me. 'Is it because I snapped at you earlier? I'm sorry about that. You know I'm not at my best when I'm hungry. Dinner wasn't your fault; I should have helped you cook instead of sitting on the sofa. I am sorry. But let's not let it ruin our night, yeah? Here, come on, sit down and have some pizza.'

Mark helps me into my chair and smiles at me before going to the fridge to sort out drinks, and as I watch him work, I feel utterly exhausted at how unpredictable he is. But that means I'm too exhausted to argue or even consider discussing what happened tonight any further, so I just sit quietly and eat my first slice of pizza, the hot tasty food helping with my hunger if not my state of mind.

Mark wastes no time in tucking into his pizza too, and as he chats excitedly about what he has planned for us tomorrow, namely a lazy Sunday beginning with a long lie-in and ending with a roast dinner at a local pub, I allow my mind to drift far away from here. It does so easily, and when it lands on a new thought, it is the couple from the wedding shop I see. Or maybe it's just him, the handsome man who was helping his fiancée find a dress. That handsome, attentive, loving man who would never treat me like Mark does.

I wish I were having pizza with him tonight.

I wish I could see him again.

But how?

I don't know anything about him. Not his name, his address, his occupation. Nothing. After leaving that pub earlier, I never expected to be able to see him or his pretty wife again, and I guess I'm correct in that assumption.

But just as I'm about to take a bite of my second slice of pizza, I have an idea.

Maybe there is a way I can see that man again.

It is a bit of a long shot, and I'm not sure it can work, but I feel like I want to give it a try, and why not?

Everyone thinks I'm happy, and for a little while when I was watching that man earlier, I guess I was. So why not try to get that feeling again and see where it might lead?

A better life for me?

A happier one?

It can't hurt to try to find out.

Can it?

6

True to his word, which is saying a lot, Mark ensured we had a lovely Sunday together, the lie-in and the roast dinner he promised me going as planned. It was one of those days where I could almost convince myself that everything was going to be alright and that I wasn't making a mistake in preparing to marry him. But that nagging voice still lingered at the back of my mind to remind me that not everything was quite right in my life and that, because of that, I should be on edge and keep my options open regarding any opportunities to potentially be happier.

I am going to listen to that voice, and that is why, as Monday morning dawns, I am going to alter my routine and do something different today.

I'm not going to go to work.

I'm going to go and do some investigating instead.

'Have a good day, love,' I say to Mark just before he kisses me goodbye and walks out of the front door with his brief-case in hand. I normally begin my commute a few minutes after him, but, today, I won't be making the journey to my office. To ensure that, I make a quick call to speak to my manager.

'I'm really sorry, Claire, but I'm afraid I'm not going to make it in today,' I say, making sure to speak quietly and then coughing a couple of times for good measure. 'I'm not feeling well. Hopefully it's just a twenty-four-hour thing and I'll be back in tomorrow.'

I know I'm not the first person in human history to fake illness to get out of going to work on a Monday, but I hope I can join the millions of people who have successfully been able to pull it off in their time. Fortunately, I do, and as I end the call whilst coughing once more to really sell it, I know I've done the first thing I needed to do today.

But that was merely the easy part.

What comes next might be much harder to accomplish.

Looking outside to make sure that Mark has definitely left, I see the empty space on our driveway, and that means I can leave the house now without worrying about seeing him again until tonight. He doesn't know that I'm not going to work today, nor do I want him to find out because that will only lead to questions, and there are no good answers I could give him to any of those at this time.

Putting on my coat, I activate the house alarm before stepping outside. It looks like rain today, and despite it supposedly being closer to summer than it was a couple of days ago, the heat of Saturday feels a long way away at present. I do hope nobody has their wedding planned for this week because the forecast has taken a sudden turn for the worse, and that would be unlucky.

Buttoning up my coat as I walk, I make my way to the train station, and there I join the throngs of commuters rushing to catch their train. But it feels good, if a little strange, to not actually be a commuter myself today, and as I step onto my train, I feel thrilled, as if I'm on some secretive mission and only I know of its existence. I suppose that is the case in a way, and as the train heads into London, I think about how I was so oblivious the last time I made this journey.

Back then, less than forty-eight hours ago, I was just a woman on her way to find a wedding dress in a shop. But today, I am a woman on her way to find the man she saw in that wedding dress shop.

I doubt the presenters of Marriage Mayhem have recorded a podcast episode covering this particular topic.

The train arrives in the city centre in good time and delivers a load of office workers to the various high-rise blocks that stand tall in this part of the city. But I walk away from all of them, and the farther I go, the quieter the streets become. It's after 9 a.m. now, which means most people are at their desks, and as the pavements clear, my mind does too.

After crossing a couple more streets and praying that the dark clouds above my head don't suddenly dump a load of rain on top of me, I finally arrive at my destination, and as I open the door and step inside, I see a familiar face appearing right on cue to greet me.

'Kate? Hi! Back so soon? I wasn't aware you had made an appointment?'

I smile at Chrissy, who is standing in front of the racks of white dresses she spent a large portion of Saturday after-noon showing me.

'Hi. No, I don't have an appointment. Sorry, is that okay? Maybe I should have called ahead?'

'No, it's fine. We don't tend to be too busy on a Monday morning.'

That seems to be an understatement, because we're the only two people in the shop, and as the rain starts to fall outside, I expect there won't be too many other people in a rush to come here anytime soon.

'So how can I help you?' Chrissy asks, and as I look past her, I see a half-eaten bacon roll on her desk as well as a cup of coffee and a magazine.

'Sorry, have I interrupted your breakfast?' I ask, knowing how annoying that can be.

'No, it's fine. Don't worry about it. I'm not supposed to be eating in here, but screw it; my manager isn't in today. *Again.*'

I get the impression Chrissy is not a big fan of her boss, and sure enough, she is only too keen to elaborate.

'Maybe if she ever came here herself and did some work, then she would realise that I don't get much chance to take breaks, so I have to eat when I can,' she goes on. 'But no, I'm the one who is here all the time, working late, working weekends, unpacking boxes, hanging dresses, and so on and so forth.'

Chrissy sounds like she needed to get that off her chest, and after she takes a deep breath, she apologises and puts her professional face back on.

'Enough about my woes; how can I help you? Have you seen a dress you like?'

'Yes, I have, actually,' I say, marking the momentous occasion with a wide grin.

'Oh, great. I was worried you hadn't been able to find anything on Saturday. So which one was it?'

'Well, it's a little awkward. I'm not sure how to explain.'

Chrissy looks suitably intrigued, and as she picks up her

coffee cup, I look around the shop and pretend to be as confused as I'm trying to sound.

'The thing is, there was another woman in here on Saturday at the same time as me, and I saw her try on a dress. It looked beautiful, and I was hoping to try it on myself. But I'm not sure which one it is.'

I gesture to the hundreds of dresses on display to illustrate my point, but as I had hoped, Chrissy knows a quick way to solve that problem.

'Let me see, what time were you in here on Saturday?' she asks, but she's talking to herself more than wanting me to answer her because she has picked up her booking diary and is now thumbing through it. That's exactly what I hoped she would do, and as I take a seat opposite her, I watch her turn back a couple of pages until she finds what she is looking for.

'Kate Allen?'

'Yep.'

'Here we are. You had a twelve noon appointment.'

'That's right.'

'Okay, let's just see who else was in here at the same time.'

'I think they came in a little after me,' I make sure to point out.

'Ahh yes, I see we had an appointment at half twelve. It was the couple. I should have remembered that. Not very often we get a man in here with his partner.'

I smile, pleased that she is on the right track now, and I wonder if she is going to tell me either of the names of the people whom I shared this shop with on Saturday. But she doesn't do that. What she does do is move her finger across the page before finding the note she scribbled down regarding the dress that the couple ordered.

'Here we are,' Chrissy says. 'It was the Beau Bridal A-Line. A beautiful dress. But I'm not sure if we have any more in stock. I'll have to check.'

'No problem.'

Chrissy gets up from her seat then and heads through a door at the back of the shop, and when it closes behind her, I take my chance.

Reaching out and turning the diary around, I find the part of the page that lists the name of the woman who had the appointment at 12:30.

Tess Nash.

But, as well as a name, I see her phone number, although that isn't much use to me. But what is of use is what's written beneath that. It's an address.

I see the words *Order Confirmation* above it, and I guess Tess had to give her details for where the dress was to be sent when it was ready, but I'm grateful for that, and with Chrissy not back yet, I take out my phone and snap a photo of that address for future reference.

Once I've got that, I'm just about to put the diary back where it was when Chrissy left it before I notice one more thing written near Tess's name.

W/D – 26th July

I guess that is her wedding day.

Surprisingly, it seems Tess left finding her perfect dress almost as late as me, and armed with that information, I turn the diary back around and put my phone away, trying to look as normal as possible before Chrissy comes back.

It's five minutes before the door to the back room opens again, and when it does, Chrissy is empty-handed.

'I'm sorry. I had a look, but we don't have another one in stock right now. But I might be able to get it ordered in for you so you can try it on then?'

'If you could, that would be great. Thank you.'

Chrissy sits back down and picks up her pen, and as she asks me for a few details, I watch her making a new entry in the diary.

'Okay, we'll give you a call as soon as we can have the dress here,' Chrissy tells me as I thank her and go to leave. I notice Chrissy pick up her bacon sandwich as I make my exit and think about how it must be quite boring for her to have to sit in this shop all day, mostly on her own, hoping for somebody to walk in and distract her for a little while. But as I walk away down the street, my thoughts move away from Chrissy and onto Tess.

Not only do I know her name now, but I know when her wedding day is and what dress she ordered, and more specifically what dress her partner seemed so impressed by.

But I know something else too.

I know her address.

And, seeing as I have the rest of the day free, I might as well go and have a quick look at her place, hadn't I?

7

A fter entering Tess's address into the map on my phone, I decided to take a taxi to her house because there didn't seem to be any tube stations nearby. But what the area lacks in good transport links, it more than makes up for in prestige. As I stare out of the window of the taxi as we get closer, the houses seem to get bigger and the cars on the driveways seem to get more expensive.

There is no doubt about it. I am in an affluent part of London now, but to make sure that fact isn't lost on me, my driver decides to pass comment.

'I tell you what, I'd love to know what all the people who live around here do for work,' the man says in a strong Cockney accent.

'Yeah, me too,' I reply as we pass a set of black gates behind which sits a large Tudor-style property that has to cost at least £3 million by my humble estimates.

'Probably a load of bankers or lawyers, I bet,' the taxi driver goes on, only a slight hint of disgust in his voice. 'Or maybe footballers. There's bound to be a few of them around here, I'm sure.'

'Yeah, maybe,' I say as a black SUV passes us by on the other side of the road, its windows tinted, which I thought was illegal, but then again, I doubt there are many police officers around here waiting to catch people breaking the law.

High property prices and low crime rates – welcome to the wealthy part of the city.

I feel my phone vibrate in my hand as we drive on, and when I look down, I see that Mark has sent me a message. It's one that should make me smile, and it almost does before I remember that he's always friendly whenever he texts me, and that is just another part of his deception.

> Hey babe. Hope you're having a good day at work. Can't wait to see you tonight. Love you xxx

I decide not to reply right now. Mark clearly has no idea what I'm really up to at this moment in time. Then again, nor do I. Is this really a good idea to come here? What am I hoping to get out of it? So I saw a man in a shop, found him attractive and followed him and, by the time I walked away, decided that he was the model fiancé and the perfect man. It's silly, though it might actually be true, but does that mean I should be doing whatever I can to see him again? I have to suspect the answer to that question is no, but I have other reasons for being here beyond wanting to learn more about that man in the wedding shop and, by extension, his wife-to-be. I know I wouldn't be doing this if I were happy in my own relationship, and as I put my phone away, I know I wouldn't be here if my fiancé treated me better.

What harm can it really do for me to come here today? I can't see a problem at all, not unless Mark or my manager at work find out – and that won't happen.

So relax, Kate, and see how this plays out.

Based on how close the little red dot on my phone's map is getting to my intended destination, I figure I am almost there, so I ask the driver if he could stop here and let me out.

'No problem,' he says before telling me the fare, and I hand him enough cash to settle the bill while leaving him with a little extra left over by way of a tip.

Getting out of the taxi, I wait until it's driven away before I start walking down the street, noticing as I do just how quiet it is around here. It's a far cry from the area where I live, where I can hear trains rumbling along the tracks in the distance as well as the sound of sirens drifting over from the inner city. It's peaceful here, and as I turn onto a clean, tree-lined street, I think about how this would be the perfect place to raise a family. Big gardens for the kids to play in, not much traffic on the roads, meaning they could ride their bicycles up and down without cars being a huge worry, and, best of all, you could be pretty confident that the neighbours were law-abiding, upstanding citizens and very different to the unknown array of characters who reside in the various residences near me.

Is that next on the agenda for Tess and her partner? A child after the wedding? One first, then maybe a second coming along a couple of years later? The perfect family unit to go with their perfect house.

How do I know their house is perfect?

Because I'm now standing right in front of it.

After double-checking with the map on my phone, I see that I am definitely in the right place, and confirming that, I walk over and stand behind one of the big willow trees by the road so that I'm out of sight of anybody who might be in the house at present.

Somebody is home, because I can see a car on the drive.

Peering out from my hiding place, my eyes move across the many windows in the house opposite, and I suppose I'm hoping to catch a glimpse of the man I saw in the shop on Saturday. But the chances of me catching him walking past a window or pausing to look out of one before carrying on with his day are remote, and besides, it might not be him who is home anyway. That could be Tess's car, and that would be disappointing because I'd rather see him than her. Or maybe neither of them are here and that vehicle belongs to their cleaner, although that's unlikely based on how expensive it looks.

The house itself is a two-storey, stone structure with a gravel driveway and a double garage. Two baskets filled with colourful flowers hang by the front door just above a white sculpture of a man holding a pot on the doorstep. I'd love to know how many bedrooms the house has, and if I had to guess from here, I'd say at least four. There are probably at least three bathrooms as well, presumably a small one downstairs and a couple upstairs, including an ensuite, and while I can't see behind the house, I bet the garden is massive.

This is clearly an expensive home that fits right in with the others in this area, and like the man who drove me here, I'd love to know what the people who live here list as their occupations. I only grow more curious when I see the front door open and Tess step out of the house.

It might be a Monday morning, but she doesn't look like a woman who is hard at work, and I get that impression because she is wearing what can only be described as gym attire. Her slender torso is partially covered by a sports bra, while a pair of leggings cover her slim bottom half. There is no doubt about it.

This is a woman who is more than ready to wow a crowd in her wedding dress.

But it seems that she isn't resting on her laurels just yet, and as the doors to the double garage open, I see that the garage itself is not used for parking vehicles or storing garden equipment but is the setting for what looks like an expensively assembled home gym. There is a treadmill in there, as well as a couple of weight machines, a few dumb-bells on a rack and a medicine ball, which is the first piece of workout equipment that Tess seems to be using today.

As I watch her slowly raise the medicine ball above her head before lowering into a squat, it's clear by how she moves that she is no stranger to physical exertion. She is making those movements look easy, movements that for me would prove downright difficult, if not impossible. I don't ever remember squatting that low before, nor can I recall the last time I lifted a heavy object above my head, but Tess is well into her workout now while I linger out here, feeling fatter and less energetic by the second.

It's not long before Tess turns her attention to the tread-mill, and as she begins jogging, I see her swinging her arms out in front of her, her posture perfect as her legs race to keep up with the speeding conveyor belt below her feet. Her blonde hair is tied into a ponytail that bobs around at the back of her head while her eyes are locked on a spot on the wall ahead of her, making her look super-focused, or 'in the zone' as athletes like to call it. I try to guess what it is she is thinking about as she runs, wondering if wedding plans are on her mind or if she has some number that she is determined to hit on the scales and can see nothing more than that in her mind as she keeps forcing her body to exert itself. Whatever she is thinking about, she never drops her pace, not even for a moment, making hard work look so effortless and causing me to only feel more envious.

Here is a woman who not only seems to have the perfect man, but she has the perfect life to go with it. She isn't spending her Monday morning rushing around like everybody else. She is doing something she loves at home, improving her physical and mental health while the majority of women her age are hunched over desks and getting neck ache from answering phone calls. She might not even have to work at all, a real lady of leisure, free to spend her day as she pleases, and if that's the case, I wonder what she has planned next. A shower probably, but then what? Some reading? A walk? A little sunbathing in the garden if the clouds part and the temperature increases? It must be brilliant to have those kinds of options, just like it must be brilliant to be getting married to a man like the one she lives in that perfect house with.

Where is he now?

He must be at work. He must be the one who pays for the lifestyle Tess enjoys. He is giving this woman everything she wants.

Why did I end up with Mark? Why couldn't I have met this guy instead? If I had, then I would be the one working out in that gym now, motivated to get myself fit because I wanted to look good for a man who already had that part of things taken care of. Instead, I'm standing out here on the street like a stalker, unhappy with my life and feeling like I'm trapped.

Tess and I have something in common.

We're both getting married.

But we also have another thing in common, something a little less innocent.

We both want to get married to the same man.

8

I loitered outside Tess's house for far too long, long enough for her to complete her workout and go back inside her house, presumably to take a shower before sitting down to enjoy a healthy salad or something similar. There was one point where the thought crossed my mind that I could try to sneak up to the property and have a look through a few of the windows, potentially getting a glimpse of what the inside of the house looked like. But that seemed a little extreme, even for me, so I walked away, and once I had retreated far enough from the house, I ordered myself another taxi and returned to my home.

But my interest in Tess Nash and her partner did not stop there.

Armed with her name, I was able to type it into the search bar of various social media websites and go on the hunt for any kind of profile page she might have. There aren't many people in the world now who don't have some kind of presence online, and, sure enough, Tess was just like everybody else. She had Facebook and Instagram accounts, and thanks to those particular sites and the way they encourage their users to share almost every aspect of their life with others, I was able to see one very telling thing.

I could see the name of the man she was in a relationship with.

Tristan.

Once I'd found him, I didn't care to look at his partner anymore, and within seconds, I was educating myself on all things Tristan Thomas, which is what I'm still doing now as the afternoon turns into early evening.

His holiday photos. His friend photos. His photos with Tess. I'm scrolling through them all, and the more I do, the more I am attracted to this man. He looked good in the dress shop, but he's photogenic too, meaning he looks just as good, if not better, in the images here.

Seeing multiple images of him with Tess makes me wish that I were the woman in the photo, just as much as I wished that I were the one walking hand in hand down the street with my loving partner or sitting in a pub having an enjoyable meal without any fear of an argument breaking out.

A little more research allows me to discover that Tristan works as a copywriter for an advertising firm in London, a fact that only makes this man even more appealing in my eyes because he is a creative. I like the thought of him using his imagination to pay his bills, doing a fun job rather than a mundane one, and that, combined with his good looks, is probably why this guy is such a catch. I bet Tess couldn't believe her luck when she got with him, although I'm sure he was feeling the same way because she is clearly no loser herself.

I can't help but think about how different my life would be if I were Tess. No psychological abuse for one thing, not to mention a bigger house, easier lifestyle and so on. I bet their wedding is going to be better than mine too. But there is one thing I might be able to have that she does too.

The same dress.

Chrissy interrupts my online stalking by phoning to tell me that she can get me the dress I need and that, while it won't be in tomorrow, it should be available to try on next week. That is one more week closer to my big day, which means I'm cutting things even more fine than I am already by waiting until then, but I tell her that it's no problem and I'll try the dress on then. I'm already pretty set on wearing that dress for my wedding now, if only because Tess will be wearing the same one, and for at least a few seconds of that day, I might be able to imagine that I am her with my perfect life as I get married to the perfect man.

The phone call ends, and it seems to have been the interruption I needed to snap me out of whatever trance I have been in all day. This fantasising has to stop. I am not Tess, and I am not marrying Tristan, and therefore, I need to stop following them, scouring their online profiles and, most of all, stop thinking about them.

That might be easier said than done, but I'm determined to focus on my own life and not someone else's, so I try to occupy myself by making dinner for Mark before he arrives home from work. Unlike last time, I'm not going to make a mess of this. I'm going to concentrate and cook the food properly, and that way, Mark can't get annoyed at me, nor can I feel like I might have let him down.

But even being busy doesn't mean Tess and Tristan don't infiltrate my thoughts on occasion but rather than let the idea of their happiness get me down, I try to use them as motivation. I imagine how good a cook Tess is and use it to spur me on to work better in the kitchen. I also imagine the kinds of details she might add to help the ambience in the house ahead of her partner coming back. I'm thinking she probably puts a little music on, opens a bottle of red wine and maybe even lights a few candles.

So that's exactly what I'm going to do.

As I do all those things and the meal gets closer to completion, I wonder if it was a good thing that I saw Tess and Tristan in the first place. Forget me having a silly crush on him or being jealous of her. I can use them for good. I can be a better fiancée and, pretty soon, a better wife, and perhaps I can even shape Mark and make him better too. I know the basic belief is that nobody should have to change themselves for another person, but that's not very realistic, is it? The fact is, relationships and especially marriages are all about compromise and altering behaviours to make life easier for both parties, so why should I be afraid of changing? I should also not be afraid to try to change Mark, although I'll have to do it in a subtle way so that he doesn't notice what I'm trying to do. And, ultimately, why should I be afraid of being better?

My mood has improved considerably by the time Mark walks through the front door, and I'm quickly on hand to greet him, delivering a glass of wine to him and telling him that dinner is about to be served. He looks surprised that I'm being this attentive, but he accepts the wine, and as he takes a sip, I give him a wink before sauntering back into the kitchen and finishing up the cooking.

I sway my hips to the soft music that's playing at a low volume while the flame from the candle sways a little in the breeze as Mark walks in and takes a seat at the table in front of the place setting I laid out for him ten minutes ago.

'What's going on?' he asks, clearly confused as to why everything seems to be so perfect and easy when it's usually a little more difficult than this.

'Nothing. I'm just in a good mood,' I say. 'The wedding's getting closer, I'm about to marry the man of my dreams, and guess what, I've found the dress I want.'

'You have?'

'Yep. It's perfect.'

'Expensive?'

That's a good question. I didn't actually ask Chrissy how much it was. Oops. But I can't let that spoil the moment.

'Don't worry about that. We have enough in the budget. How was your day at work?'

I change the subject quickly before Mark can ask me any more about the dress or that budget, the latter of which might not quite have as much left in it as I need. But my tactic doesn't quite do the trick.

'Kate, how much is the dress?'

'I haven't bought it yet.'

'Okay, but you obviously like it. So how much is it?'

'I don't know.'

'How can you not know?'

'Well, I haven't tried it on yet.'

'So? You can still look at the price tag or ask the assistant how much it is, can't you?'

'I guess.'

'So why haven't you?'

There really is no simple way I can answer Mark's question honestly without sounding like a complete weirdo. Somehow, I don't think telling him that I have ordered a dress without checking the price and all because I saw another woman wearing it is a sensible response.

But, unfortunately, my silence doesn't help me much either.

'For God's sake, Kate, what is wrong with you?' Mark asks, getting up from the table and almost knocking over his glass of wine in the process. 'First, you take forever to find a dress, something that has annoyed me for a long time and you know it. But then you find one only to tell me that you have no idea how much it costs, so how can you know we can even afford it?'

'We will be able to afford it.'

'How? Because I'll just pay for it? Well, thanks, I love working hard all day so you can spend all my money for me.'

'Mark! That is not what I do!'

'It feels like it sometimes!'

The romantic song playing quietly in the background seems absurd now as the pair of us stand opposite each other in the midst of yet another damn disagreement.

'Do you even want to get married to me?' I ask. 'Do I even make you happy? Because if I do, then you have a funny way of showing it.'

'Not this again. How many times do I have to convince you that I want to marry you? Do you think I just tripped up and landed on one knee the day I proposed? Don't ask such stupid questions; it's not a good look for you.'

I feel like picking up one of the plates I set out on the table in anticipation of a romantic meal and hurling it at Mark's head. Sure, he might duck out of the way, but it will still be satisfying to see it smash against the wall behind him, and I know it will definitely give him pause for thought. But it won't help cool this situation down, nor will it go any way towards helping me convince myself that I shouldn't just leave and never come back.

'Look, we just need to get to this wedding, and then once we're married, things will be easier,' Mark says.

'How will they be easier?' I ask, hoping that he has a really good answer for me that will put my mind at ease.

'You'll see it's a good thing to be a wife. Look at the wives of my friends. They are all happy. They know how to behave. My friends have no problems with them, and soon, we'll be the same.'

And here we have the one area where Mark and I are so very similar. I stay with him because I want to keep up appearances with my friends, and, likewise, he is marrying me because he wants to do the same with his. All his mates have loyal, obedient partners, and I know that's all he cares about. To hell with whether these women are actually happy or not; they just do as they are told while the men do as they please. He wants that for us too. I know it. But what can I do about it?

Maybe I can fight back.

'Finish making your own dinner,' I say as I walk out of the kitchen. 'I've suddenly lost my appetite.'

I rush upstairs before Mark can stop me and lock myself in the bathroom, where I sit on the toilet and allow myself to cry. But things only get worse when I look at my phone and see that Molly has sent me a few details about the plan for the weekend. My hen do is almost here now. All the girls are excited. I can't let them down.

'Can't wait,' I say in reply to the message about Molly coming to pick me up on Saturday morning before we head to Manchester.

Then I throw my phone across the bathroom and cry some more.

9

My small suitcase is packed and sitting by the bed as I hurry back into the bathroom and make one more quick check on my appearance. There'll be plenty of time to apply more make-up and do my hair again when I get to the hotel in Manchester, but I still want to make sure I'm looking good now for all the photos that I'll be in on the way there. It's my hen weekend, and I intend to document it, and after checking my reflection in the mirror, I feel like I'm ready for all the photos and videos that I am about to be the star of.

As I leave the bathroom, I'm just about to call out to Mark and ask him if he'll give me a hand carrying my luggage down the stairs, but he's already up here, having come into the bedroom without me hearing him.

'Oh, hey. How do I look?' I ask him, giving a little twirl so he can see me and my summer dress from all angles and form an honest opinion.

'Fine,' he mumbles back before looking at my suitcase.

'What's wrong?' I ask him because it's obvious he's not in

a great mood, but I already knew that with how he's been with me since we woke up this morning. He hasn't told me what's bothering him yet, but I have a feeling I know what it is.

He's not as excited about me going for a night away with the girls as I am.

'Nothing,' he says as he glances at my suitcase.

'I'm not going to do anything stupid,' I say with a smile. 'Yes, I'll be drinking champagne, and yes, the girls can get pretty wild, but I'll be fine.'

'You think? Molly can be a bad influence.'

'She's my best friend. She's always looking out for me.'

'Is she?'

'What do you mean?'

'Just don't drink too much. Don't stay out too late. Behave yourself.'

'Yes, Dad,' I say, but I regret my quip instantly when Mark frowns.

Thankfully, a knock at the front door interrupts us. I guess it's Molly coming to pick me up.

'Can you help with my suitcase?' I ask Mark, but he's already leaving the room, so I pick it up myself and haul it to the stairs.

Mark is already at the bottom of it, but just before he opens the door, he waits for me to join him. I almost drop the suitcase at his feet by the time I do, because it wasn't exactly an easy thing to get downstairs.

I'm annoyed he didn't help me with it, but there's no time for me to say anything now as he opens the door, and when he does, I see Molly on the other side holding a pink sash and a *Bride-To-Be* balloon.

'There she is! Hello, hen! I hope you're ready for a crazy weekend!'

Molly is practically bursting with excitement and does a jiggle on the spot before rushing forward to give me a hug.

I hug her back, squeezing her tightly because I'm so grateful for her and all the work she has put into this weekend, work that can't have been easy to do while she was busy juggling her hectic home life that consists of a husband, two kids and three – yes, three – chihuahuas.

No sooner have we separated than Mark is going in for a hug of his own from Molly.

'Hey, Molly, you look well,' he says with a beaming smile.

'Thank you, Mark. You too!'

'So what exciting things have you planned for my fiancée?' he asks as he releases her from the hug.

'Oh, that would be telling, wouldn't it,' Molly replies with a laugh before suggesting we get a move on so we can go and meet the other girls at the train station.

'Here, let me get that for you,' Mark says as he reaches down and picks up my suitcase, something he didn't want to do a moment ago but is clearly keen to do now we have company. As he carries my luggage to the waiting taxi, I let out a sigh.

He's always like this, always on top form whenever anybody else is around. The way he greeted Molly so enthusiastically makes him look like a friendly guy, and the way he's carrying my suitcase makes it look like he's a gentleman, but it's funny how different he was before my friend got here. He was basically saying he doubted that she had my best interests at heart, yet no sooner did he see her than he couldn't wait to give her a hug.

Why does he have to be like this?

Why can't he be the happy, charming, gentlemanly guy all the time?

Why can't he be like Tristan?

'Have a great time! Don't forget to send me a message to let me know you're still alive!' Mark says with a laugh as he waves at Molly and me as we get into the back of the taxi. 'I love you!'

'Love you too,' I call to him before I close my door, and no sooner have I done that than Molly is telling me how great Mark is and how lucky I am to have him.

'Yeah,' I say quietly as I wave at my fiancé before he disappears from view and the taxi leaves our street.

We spend the ten-minute journey to the station excitedly chatting about all the fun we are going to have and how quickly time has gone since we first set the date for this hen party, and by the time the taxi stops again, I have forgotten about my problems with Mark. Seeing the rest of my friends only helps me forget even more, and once we've all boarded our train, I'm feeling fantastic.

There are nine of us here, and we are meeting another friend in Manchester, and as our train moves through the countryside, we're all in great spirits, so much so that I feel a little sorry for some of the other people in our carriage. A few of my friends have never been quiet at the best of times, but now we're fully into party mode, the decibel levels have gone up a couple of notches.

'Woo! I love you girls! This is going to be the best weekend!'

'Kate, I can't believe you're finally tying the knot! About time!'

'This weekend is going to be crrrrazzzzy!'

My face is hurting from smiling so much, and we're not

even halfway to Manchester yet, a city I picked as the location for my hen party because it's one of the few cities in the UK that hadn't already been used by the rest of my friends when they had their own parties. Being the last one in the friendship group to marry meant that a lot of the places I might have considered would have seemed slightly anticlimactic if we'd already been there before, not that anyone would have complained too much if I'd chosen the same place as someone else. But Manchester was still untested, so I went with that one, and as we speed towards it, I am looking forward to a change of scene. I'm also looking forward to the distraction from wedding planning, but that might be a little harder to achieve because everybody I'm with has plenty of questions to ask me about things, starting with the dreaded dress.

'Have you found one yet, Kate? Please tell me that you have!'

Eight anxious faces look back at me as I sit in my seat by the window, holding a can of gin and tonic. They all know the arduous search I have been on to find the right dress to wear. But, fortunately, I have some good news.

'Actually, I have,' I reply, and that answer is met by several squeals of delight.

'Oh my God! What did you choose? You have to show us! Have you got photos?'

'Er, I don't have a photo on my phone. I haven't been able to try it on yet, but I should be able to next week,' I say as the train curves round a bend in the track.

'What's it called? We should be able to find it online,' Molly asks me before jokingly admonishing me for having found a dress but keeping quiet about it.

I give her the name of the design, and while she types

that into her phone, I watch as two of the girls rummage around in a shopping bag before taking out some snacks for us to nibble on during our journey.

'Hey, I'm supposed to be on a diet!' I say, but that doesn't stop me from scoffing a few cheese and onion crisps.

'Oh my gosh. Is it this one?' Molly asks me, and she turns her phone around to show me the dress she's found online.

I check the image; it looks right, so I nod.

'Yeah, that's it. What do you think?' I ask, eager for my friend's opinion. I'm sure she'll love it. It really is a gorgeous dress.

'I mean, don't get me wrong, it's beautiful,' Molly says, and she shows the dress to the rest of the girls, who all agree that it really is. 'But what I want to know is how the hell did you get Mark to allow you to spend so much money on it?'

Everybody looks at me, their expressions a mixture of awe and envy, but I'm not quite sure what they mean. That's because I still don't actually know how much the dress costs.

'Why, how much does it say it is there?' I ask, pretending to want to check if the price listed online is different to the price I was given in the shop. But, of course, I wasn't given a price in the shop because I didn't ask, so this is going to be the first time I get any idea of its cost. As I take the phone, I make sure to take a deep breath.

That's when I understand why Molly and the rest of my friends are so in awe of me.

I can now see how much the dress costs, and it's bad.

It's really bad.

'Seriously, Kate, what's your secret?' Molly asks. 'I mean, unless you won the lottery or something? Have you? Maybe you have, you lucky girl!'

I really should answer her or at least look up from this

phone to acknowledge that I heard her. But I don't. I just keep staring at the number on the screen, but no matter how hard I look at it, it doesn't get any smaller.

£6,000

How could I have been so stupid as to think I'd found the right dress without checking the price? And how could I have been so stupid as to not realise that a woman as obviously as wealthy as Tess is would always be paying a high figure for her wedding dress? She was hardly going to pick something from the bargain basket, was she? Not when she lives in that house. Spending this kind of money might be a drop in the ocean for her, but this is way out of my price range, and there's no way I'll be able to afford it.

Is there?

'I still have to try it on yet, so I'm not getting carried away,' I tell my friends, so at least I have a way out of this if I do decide to back out. I can just say that I tried it on, but it wasn't quite right, and that will be the end of it. But do I want to do that? What if there is a way that I could still have this dress? I have some savings. Would it be a stupid thing to do to spend it all on this one thing for this one day?

'What did Mark say when you told him how much it was?' Molly asks me, still shaking her head in disbelief that my wedding dress might be about to cost so much more than hers did.

'Oh, erm, he was a little surprised,' I say. 'But, you know, I'm working on him, and I'm sure he'll be alright about it in the end.'

The girls laugh before raising their drinks and telling me how amazing I am for being able to get my fiancé to agree that we should part with so much money for a wedding dress.

'He must love you so much!' one of them cries, but I'm not sure who said that because I'm back to looking at the phone again. I'm not looking at the price this time. I'm looking at the photo of the dress instead.

This is a dress that Tristan thinks is beautiful, and for some reason, his opinion matters to me.

That's why I have to have it, even if nothing else ever comes of it.

But who says it won't?

10

Manchester has not disappointed us. Brushing off my shock over how much my wedding dress might end up costing me, I made sure to fully throw myself into all the celebrations that my friends have organised for me. And what a time I have had doing so.

After arriving in the city, we linked up with the last member of the group to join us before I was whisked away to a fancy restaurant, where we had an incredible lunch, gorging on sumptuous seafood and washing it all down with some wonderful white wine. After that it was onto a cocktail-making class, where we were all taught how to create various drinks by a very handsome French guy wearing a bow tie, a pair of tight black trousers and very little else. From there, we went to the hotel, where we all put our finest dresses on and reapplied our make-up before heading out for more food. That's been followed by a string of venues that have gradually become slightly less classy as we moved amongst them. While we were in trendy wine bars earlier in the night, we have been in various questionable places since, and now, as the clock approaches 2 a.m., we find ourselves singing on a crowded dance floor in some underground nightclub.

We might not be twenty anymore, but we sure are acting like it.

My friends are clearly making the most of having a night away from their normal responsibilities, emboldened by the alcohol and free from having to do menial chores like nappy changing, bedtime stories and various bits of housework. But they have all made sure to tell me just how wonderful marriage can be and that I'm going to be even happier when I become a wedded woman.

'If you love your partner now, wait until you get to call them hubby!'

'It's so nice to get married. I wish I could do it all over again!'

'Get the wedding out of the way, and then you can move on to the easy stuff. Kids! Ha!'

It might have felt a little overwhelming if not for the fact that I'm relaxed by all the food and drink I've consumed today, and as I hold my hands high above my head and dance to the latest song from the DJ in the booth, I feel free. But, as always, good feelings don't last forever, and by the time we stagger out of the club and onto the chilly street, my mood has dipped somewhat. I'm tired, feeling a little nauseous, and, most of all, that feeling of freedom I had earlier has vanished.

If anything, I'm now starting to panic that I might be trapped.

Molly seems to notice the change in my mood after we have made it back to the hotel and several of the girls have disappeared off to their rooms.

'Everything okay?' she asks as we enter the room we are

sharing together, and a little voice in my head tells me then that this could be my opportunity to let my best friend know that I'm not as happy as I pretend to be. But it's not the right time. It's the early hours of the morning, we're both drunk, and I know I'll regret saying anything when I wake up. And that's without considering the fact that it would be awful of me to tell Molly that I'm having second thoughts about Mark being the one for me after she's just spent all day giving me an incredible send-off into married life.

'Yeah, all good. I'm just exhausted,' I say as I pull my heels off my aching feet and slump onto one of the twin beds. 'I haven't danced like that in years.'

'And you probably never will again,' Molly says with a laugh. 'This time next year, you'll be waddling around with a baby bump. Or you might already be up to your elbows in nappies by then.'

'One thing at a time,' I say, dismissing the idea in a light-hearted way before peeling off my dress and putting my pyjamas on. But that's more than Molly can manage. When I look over at her, she's fallen asleep still in her dress, passed out on top of her duvet and snoring away, leaving me to cover her in a blanket, turn off the lights and set the alarm for the morning.

I try not to think too much about the reality that we have to be up in only a few short hours to check out of this hotel, but before I close my eyes and try to get some sleep, I decide to do a little scrolling around on social media. But really, there's only one thing my inebriated brain wants to look at, and before I know it, I'm on Tristan's Instagram page.

I should put my phone down and get some rest, but I can't stop looking at all the various photos that Tristan has uploaded over the years. The more recent images seem to suggest a mature man, very much ready to settle down. There are several of him out hiking with Tess or a couple of friends, showing how he likes to get out and enjoy the great outdoors on his weekends. I guess his clubbing days have been over for a while too. There are also a few photos of cappuccinos or other forms of coffee that look like they have been taken in artisan places where people go when they want to spend a little more money to get their caffeine fix, proving further that he has moved on from consuming less healthy drinks.

But as I scroll down his page and find the older posts, I get the full timeline of Tristan's life journey, at least in his adult years anyway, because the further I look back, the more I see the changes he has gone through, both physically and in the way he chooses to spend his free time. There is a photo from two years ago in which he looks to be sleeping on a train, and it is accompanied by the caption:

Another heavy weekend. Getting too old for this.

A photo six months before that shows him on a stag do in Bulgaria and an image two years ago displays him drinking a beer on a Thai beach with his top off, his toned abs glistening in the sun. The caption there reads:

All play and no work.

I go back still further and see just how much play Tristan enjoyed in his time, and I note that there is no sign of Tess in any of these images. I guess he met her quite recently, then, so he hasn't been settled down all that long. It seems like his hiking and coffeeshop days began when he met her, suggesting he either wanted to grow up when she came along, or she suggested he do a little growing up if he wanted her to stick around.

Before I know it, I'm a full five years back on Tristan's Instagram, looking at photos of him where he appears very fresh-faced, a youthful look that is in contrast to the slightly more rugged, mature look he had when I saw him in the dress shop.

Put the phone down and go to sleep, I tell myself as it gets later and later and the window of time before my alarm goes off shrinks more and more. Molly's snoring is getting louder too: at least one of us will have had some rest when the sun comes up over Manchester soon. But I continue to scroll, and now I'm six years back, gazing at photos of Tristan on various nights out, looking smart in shirts and with a few attractive women by his side. I guess he played the field before he proposed to Tess, but who could blame him when he looks as good as he does? I just wish I'd been one of the lucky women who encountered him on a night out, because maybe then, I'd have been the one he went and bought a ring for. If that had happened, I might not be lying in a hotel room feeling blue and scrolling through pictures of somebody who is not my fiancé.

And that's when it happens. It's an accident, but it's occurred before I have time to stop it. I've foolishly double-tapped one of Tristan's old photos, and because I have now 'liked' it, one more number is instantly added to the little hearts underneath the image to signify the people who have liked this photo. But the problem is, one, I didn't mean to do it, and two, all the people who have already liked this picture would have done so six years ago when it was first posted. But the fact that I've liked an image from 2017 when we're in

2023 now makes it massively obvious that I have been scrolling all this way back on his profile.

'No,' I say out loud as I try to 'unlike' the image, but while I achieve that quite easily, I know it's probably already too late. A notification will have been sent to Tristan's account to tell him that somebody has liked one of his photos, and when he sees it, he'll be able to see my profile. Worryingly, he will then wonder why I, a complete stranger to him, was looking at his old photos.

I'm an idiot. I've given myself away. He's going to know I'm obsessed with him, and now he'll think I'm a crazy person. Okay, so he can't come and find me and ask me why I seemed to be so fascinated with his old photos, but he'll still know that I was. That means I can never be around him again. I couldn't strike up a conversation with him one day and act like we've just met, not now I've blown my cover.

As if I managed to go to his house and successfully spy on him at home only to then go and accidentally express my interest on social media.

The only thing I can do is put my phone down and close my eyes while telling myself to forget all about Tristan. Even if there was some crazy way that I might have ended up with him in the future, that has gone now because he'll have me pegged as a stalker.

I guess that's it, then.

I guess I'll just have to stick to my original plan and marry Mark.

I guess the fantasy of me and Tristan somehow meeting, falling in love, ditching our partners at the last minute and getting married to each other instead is over.

And when I think about how crazy all of that sounds, it's probably for the best.

11

I ended up sleeping through my alarm and only woke up when Molly started shaking me.

'Kate! Oh my gosh, you're okay! I thought you were dead or something!'

Molly relaxes when she sees I've opened my eyes and shown a few more signs of life, although to say I feel 'alive' right now might be exaggerating matters somewhat. Sure, my heart is still beating, but I feel terrible. My head is pounding, my mouth is dry, my feet are aching, and when I try to remember when I got into this bed, I draw a blank.

There are bad hangovers.

And then there is this one.

'I can't believe you didn't hear the alarm,' Molly tells me as she picks up some of her belongings from the floor and throws them into her suitcase; as always she's very uncoordinated and makes a harder job of it than it should be. 'And I can't believe you didn't hear me shouting at you.'

'Urghh,' is the only sound I can manage at the moment as I put a hand to my face and close my eyes again.

'We need to get going. Remember we agreed to skip the brunch and leave early so Lucy could get back? Childcare issues. Our train is in twenty minutes,' Molly tells me, delivering the grim news before she disappears into the bathroom, and then I start to hear what sounds like retching.

This is one of those situations where a person can either laugh or cry, but seeing as this is my hen weekend and I had a great time yesterday, or at least I think I did from what I can remember of it, I choose laughter. Before I know it, I have an uncontrollable bout of giggles, and by the time Molly remerges from the bathroom, tears are actually streaming down my face because I'm laughing so hard.

'I'm glad you find this funny,' Molly says as she stops walking for a moment and holds onto the wall behind her to get her balance back. 'I'm such a mess. What are my children going to say when they see me stagger through the front door looking like this?'

That question only makes me laugh even more, and I end up wasting the little time that neither of us have.

'What time did we get in last night?' I ask before I finally haul myself out of bed and begin to pick up the pieces of my life, or in this case, the pieces of the outfit I was wearing before I hurriedly undressed and fell onto the mattress.

'I have no idea,' Molly tells me. 'I can't remember much after midnight.'

'Me neither,' I admit before giving up on picking up my clothes and instead going into the bathroom to do a little of what my best friend was doing in here only a few moments ago.

By the time the pair of us make it out of our room with our luggage in tow, we are seriously cutting it fine if we want to make our train back to London. But we're not the only ones, and my group of friends make a sorry sight when I see them languishing in the reception area, looking just as drained as Molly and me.

I'm not sure quite how we manage it, but we make it onto our train with just seconds to spare before it departs Manchester and begins to head down south. In stark contrast to our journey up here, our carriage is almost silent as we try to nurse our hangovers in peace. The only time anyone does speak is when they recall a sliver of a memory of things we might have done in the early hours of the morning, and whenever we hear about those things, every one of us winces and feels the shame that comes with knowing we were definitely wild last night. But I can't add too much to any of those conversations because I really cannot remember much beyond the last wine bar we went in. I certainly don't remember being in a nightclub, just like I can't remember getting back to the hotel. But one thing I can see is that Mark messaged me at 2 a.m. asking if I was still awake, followed by another message at 3 a.m. saying that he could see I was still active online on Instagram and Facebook, and he was wondering what I was doing.

But I didn't reply to any of his messages.

I quickly type out a text to let him know that I am fine and on the way home to him, before adding that I can't wait to see him, an addition that I hope will make him smile. But I can't shake the lingering fear that he might be mad at me for not only staying up so late last night, but not replying to his texts. I guess I won't find out what mood he is in with me for sure until I get back home.

The last thing I need in my current state is an argument, but after a very arduous two-hour train journey, followed by a taxi ride in which I was convinced I was going to have to ask the driver to pull over because I might be sick, I make it back to my front door and walk through with a great sense of trepidation. Mark did not reply to the message I sent him from the train, and that has only increased my anxiety about whether or not he is angry at me.

And then I get my answer.

It comes in the form of a stony silence. Mark does not say a word as I enter the kitchen and greet him, nor does he move much when I go to give him a hug.

As I feared, he's not happy.

'I'm sorry I didn't reply to your messages last night,' I say. 'It got a bit crazy with the girls. A few of them got really drunk, so I was looking after them.'

'You were looking after them? Or they were looking after you?'

'I was fine.'

'You don't look it. You look like death warmed up.'

'Okay, so I was out a little late.'

'A little late? I saw you were still online at three in the morning! That's more than a little late!'

'It was my hen party! What do you want me to say? That we were all tucked up in bed with a cup of hot cocoa at 9 p.m., because that's not very realistic, is it?'

'You promised me that you wouldn't get drunk and stay out late!'

'No, I didn't, and the fact you would even try to make me promise such a thing is ridiculous! Why can't you just let me enjoy myself with my friends?'

'You know why! I've told you! They're a bad influence.'

'A bad influence how? They're all loyal wives and brilliant mothers with good careers. What is wrong with any of that?'

'They don't listen to their husbands! Do you think a man likes to know that his woman is out running around some strange city in the early hours of the morning?'

'His woman? What the hell is that supposed to mean? You think you own me or something.'

'I didn't say that.'

'Whatever you said, it sounded incredibly sexist to me!'

This is the last thing I need with a headache. I turn to leave the room because I need to get out of here before this gets any worse.

'Where are you going?' Mark asks, his voice lower now, sounding meeker and milder mannered, as if he weren't just shouting at me a moment ago and can't understand why I might want to walk away.

'Upstairs!'

'Why? You've been away virtually all weekend. I want to spend time with you.'

'You've just had a go at me as soon as I got home!'

'I missed you, and I was upset you didn't reply to me. Sorry if that makes me a bad fiancé.'

'No, what makes you a bad fiancé is you criticising all my friends and, by extension, criticising me. What is it you think I did last night? That I was with some other man? That I was so drunk that I didn't know what I was doing? Is that how little you think of me?'

'No, of course not.'

'Do you even trust me?'

'Yes!'

'Then stop having a go at me!'

'Okay, I'm sorry. Kate, come here. I love you.'

Mark rushes to me then before I can leave the kitchen and hugs me tightly, though I make little effort to hug him back. My homecoming after a fun night out has been nothing short of a nightmare, and I feel drained just being in the same room as the man I'm supposed to marry.

'How about you get a shower, and then we'll go for a walk, and you can tell me all about your hen party?' Mark suggests, switching back into nice-guy mode once again. But I didn't miss the strong hint about him suggesting that I wasn't smelling great after my late night, although I'm not going to let that offend me. Right now, I can't think of anything better than locking myself in the bathroom and having a little peace and privacy.

'Okay,' I say as we separate. 'I'll go and have a shower.'

It's a relief to get upstairs, and it's an even bigger relief when I lock the bathroom door behind me and take a seat on the edge of the bathtub.

I need a moment to decompress before I undress and shower, so to do that, I go on Instagram with the plan of distracting myself with a few harmless updates from the various celebrity accounts I follow. But as soon as I open the app, I see that I have a new message, and when I click to find out who it is from, my heart almost skips a beat.

It's from Tristan.

I have no idea why he would have messaged me or how he could have even found me online, but when I read the message, it all comes flooding back to me.

Hey. Do we know each other? I saw you liked one of my photos quite late last night. It's a very old photo, actually. Have we met?

I'm mortified at the message because reading it has just given me a flashback to what I did. I was stalking Tristan's

Instagram page in the early hours of the morning when I accidentally liked a photo of his from six years ago.

Six years! That's so embarrassing!

Oh my God, he saw it, and now he thinks I'm a total weirdo. Well done, Kate, you've unnerved this man and forced him to try to find out if you're a psycho.

My first thought is to ignore the message. Delete it and move on. Forget all about it. But doing that won't answer Tristan's questions, and if I ignore him, he will just assume I was some sad woman looking at photos of an attractive guy online. I need to say something back. I need to respond to him in a way that makes me seem less of a freak and more of a normal person.

But what can I say? There is no reason for me to have liked that photo without having trawled back through hundreds of them. How can I spin this so it seems like an innocent mistake.

And then I have it, an idea coming to me through my fog of fatigue.

Hey! Sorry for liking the photo. It was an accident. I was looking back that far because I thought I recognised you as someone I went to school with. I was trying to see if I could find a photo of you when you were younger, so I would know if it was you or not. But I think I got mixed up. No worries!

I press send and hope that will work, but no sooner have I done that than I see Tristan's reply.

Oh, okay. Which school did you go to?

Damn it.

Miller High School. On Green Lane.

I know Tristan won't have gone there, but I have to keep up appearances here, so I let him know the school in question.

No, I didn't go there. You must be thinking of somebody else.

That seems to have got me out of this predicament, so I'll take it.

Okay, I must be! Sorry again!

I expect that to be the end of it and feel relieved that I seem to have been able to disguise my online stalking with a somewhat plausible excuse. But then Tristan messages me again.

You know, I think I recognise you from somewhere.

I hold my breath when I read that, now terrified that he saw me following him and his partner the other day, through London and into that pub. What if he did?

Do you? I'm not sure from where haha.

I've tried to make my response light and jokey, but I'm not laughing as I wait to see what Tristan will say next.

Were you in the bridal shop on Church Street the
other day?

Oh no, he did see me. He recognises me from the shop.
Now he's going to know for sure that I've been stalking him.
What can I say to this?

Deciding that honesty might be the best policy, I say yes,
I was there. What will he say to that? Will he ask me why I
sought him out online after I saw him in that same shop?

No, he doesn't ask any more questions. He just says
something that makes me smile.

I thought it was you. I never forget a pretty face.

pretty face.

A Tristan thinks I have a pretty face. The man who is handsome and gentlemanly and a million miles out of my league thinks I have a pretty face.

What am I supposed to do with this information?

It's been five minutes since Tristan sent me his last message, and I haven't replied to it yet because I'm trying to process the mixture of feelings I have about it. On the one hand, I'm surprised that he would say such a thing to another woman when he's in a relationship with someone else. It's a little flirty, I suppose. But on the other hand, I'm extremely thrilled at two things.

One, he obviously finds me attractive.

And two, *he noticed me.*

In the end, there isn't much I can say other than what anybody should say after receiving a compliment.

Thank you.

My reply is short and sweet, because I've resisted any urge to send a compliment back to Tristan myself. Despite being aware that he has a pretty face himself, it feels wrong of me to say such a thing because then it really would be getting flirty, and is that right? We're both engaged, but I guess the main reason I didn't offer Tristan any compliment is because the thought of Mark ever seeing that I sent such a message sends a shiver down my spine. He'd be jealous and angry, but, in that case, I wouldn't be able to blame him, so I'll keep things as platonic as I can between Tristan and me for now.

But maybe that's it. Maybe there will be no more communication between me and him. As I stare at my phone to see if another message comes back, nothing happens.

I realise after a few minutes that I've already been in this bathroom a while, and I haven't had my shower yet, so I'd better do that, or Mark will be wondering what I'm up to.

Already feeling like I'm doing something wrong and keeping secrets from my fiancé, I undress and turn on the shower while thinking about Tristan and his unexpected messages. But, as I tell myself, I've not done anything wrong and shouldn't feel guilty. Tristan has messaged me and been nice, and I've replied, like any polite person should.

But the fact that the first thing I do after my shower is grab my phone again to see if he has sent any more messages tells me that I am already starting to get in deep. And what do I find?

There is a new message waiting for me.

As I stand in front of the steamed-up mirror with wet hair and a towel wrapped around my wet body, I read Tristan's latest message.

So I guess you're getting married too. Are you as
nervous as I am about it?

I smile at the question before replying to let Tristan
know that I am very nervous, and it's nice to find out that
someone else in a similar position to me feels the same way.
The truth is while everyone says a wedding is the best day of
your life, they don't mention the year or two of stress that
often precedes it, do they?

We go back and forth for a couple more minutes,
discussing or rather lamenting just how much there is to get
in place before a wedding can actually take place. But I'm
interrupted by the sound of Mark coming up the stairs, so I
quickly dry myself off and unlock the door, making sure to
keep my phone out of sight underneath a towel so he doesn't
know I've been using it.

But even doing such a simple thing tells me I'm already feeling
guilty.

'I was just coming to check you hadn't drowned in the
shower,' Mark says with a chuckle. 'You were a while in
there. Everything alright?'

'Yeah, fine! I feel much better now. Refreshed.'

'Great! Get yourself dressed, and we'll get out for some
fresh air. That'll make you feel even better.'

Mark seems very cheery as he heads back downstairs
while I rush into our bedroom and begin to get dressed. I tell
myself not to check my phone anymore, not for a little while
at least, because I can't let myself get so obsessed with
Tristan and any messages he might send. I'll be polite and
keep replying, I suppose, but I don't have to do it so quickly,
and I know I should be spending more time thinking about
the man downstairs than the man on the end of my DMs.

Having got dressed and dried my hair, I find Mark in the kitchen and see that he's looking at a holiday brochure.

'What are you doing?' I ask him.

'Just plotting,' he replies before closing the brochure and suggesting we go outside.

I'm still wondering about what he might have planned as we set off on our walk, the sky a lovely blue above our heads and the temperature just perfect, and slowly but surely my hangover is receding into the background.

'Are you thinking about another holiday?' I ask Mark when the suspense becomes too much for me. 'I mean, besides the honeymoon.'

'Maybe,' comes the mysterious answer.

Normally, that would make me very excited, because who wouldn't want to go on holiday? But that was before I found out how much the wedding dress was, and if I am to actually buy that one, I doubt there will be much money left over for a vacation. But I don't say anything to Mark about that, just happy that he is in one of his good moods, and as we make our way into the park, I have another one of my moments where I tell myself everything is going to be fine.

But that doesn't mean my mind doesn't wander to my mobile phone and, more specifically, my Instagram account, and I know that the only reason for that is because I am wondering if Tristan is still messaging me. *This is so stupid*, I think as we make our way over to an ice cream van with a short queue lined up beside it. I feel like I did when I was younger, anxiously hoping my crush would text me back and feeling like it might be the end of the world if he didn't. But of course it wouldn't be the end of the world if Tristan didn't keep messaging me because I have a lot to be grateful for. I have a fiancé, a nice home, a good job, amazing friends, and most likely one day soon, I'll be pregnant too.

So why do I feel like the only thing that could make me happy at the moment is hearing from Tristan again?

'Two scoops of vanilla, please,' Mark says to the guy in the van, and while he is distracted rummaging around in his wallet for some cash, I sneakily take the opportunity to check my messages while his back is turned. When I do, I see that there are two unread messages from Tristan waiting for me.

The first one is just another observation on the travails of wedding planning, very much along the lines of the chat we were having earlier. But the second message, sent fifteen minutes after that last one, becomes a little more personal again.

Did you find the right wedding dress? When is your big day?

Those two questions seem innocent enough on the face of it, but I can't help but wonder why Tristan is so interested in finding out the answers. But there's not enough time to send a reply because Mark turns around with my ice cream then, so I stuff my phone back into my pocket and gratefully accept the cone with its two scoops of vanilla ice cream sitting on top of it.

'Thanks. Didn't you want anything?' I ask him when I see he didn't get something for himself.

'No, I'd better not if I want to fit into my suit. But you don't have to worry about that. You'll look incredible on the day whatever you do. Enjoy.'

We walk on then, Mark holding my free hand while I use

my other one to keep the ice cream close to my mouth. But as we make a meandering path around the park, I almost feel bad that Mark is being so nice to me now. It only makes me regret replying to Tristan and seeking out a little joy there. It certainly feels much easier on my conscience to be messaging a man I'm attracted to when my current boyfriend is being so nasty to me. But now he's being nice, those messages on my Instagram account feel like they're burning away in my pocket.

Mark's pleasant demeanour lasts all the way into the evening, long after we have got back from the park and even after we have had a chicken salad for our dinner, so much so that I'm thinking we might actually go to bed on good terms for the first time in a while. But alas, I was wrong, because once again, Mark finds the smallest and silliest possible thing to snap at me over, and before I know it, he's being mean to me again.

This time he's annoyed because he has seen the hen party photos that Molly's uploaded to social media, and he has taken offence to the ones in which I look more than a little inebriated.

'Look at the state of you. Aren't you embarrassed about this?' Mark asks me as he shows me the photos on his phone and shakes his head in dismay.

'It was a night out. We were having fun.'

'But why does it have to end up splashed all over the internet?'

'It's no big deal.'

'No big deal to you maybe. But I can't say I'm the biggest fan of having my fiancée's drunken antics displayed for the whole world to see.'

I'm far too tired to argue, so I just say it wasn't my fault

Molly put the photos online. Then I get into bed, and Mark eventually does the same. But once again, I'm annoyed and saddened at my partner's behaviour, and that is why, once I'm certain he has fallen asleep beside me, I go back into my Instagram messages and reignite the conversation with Tristan.

> I have found a dress actually! Going to try it on very soon. My wedding is in three weeks, so it's all a little last minute! When is your big day?

Given that it has taken me almost six hours to reply to him, I'm not expecting Tristan to come back tonight, or maybe even at all. But I'm wrong there because he responds a minute later with his wedding date, even though I already knew it from snooping in the customer book in the shop. Then he sends a jovial message straight after it.

> I guess you're taking the plunge before me then. You'll have to let me know how married life is! Maybe I'll have time to back out if it's a bad idea!

It's all very light-hearted, but the fact he would even joke about backing out makes me wonder. Is he really convinced about getting married to Tess? Or is he having second thoughts like I am about Mark?

The more I think about it, the more I wonder what Tristan's partner would make of it if she knew her fiancé was messaging another woman, a woman who was clearly snooping at old photos of him.

Tristan has to know that I fancy him.

But then a little voice asks: *What if he fancies me?*

As Mark's snoring gets louder beside me, Tristan's messages only continue to arrive in my inbox, and as the clock ticks past midnight, the pair of us are still awake and still online.

Corresponding.

Chatting.

Connecting.

13

There's nothing that can send a person crashing back down to reality after a great weekend faster than an alarm clock going off to tell that person to get out of bed, leave the house and go to work. While Saturday night was full of champagne-fuelled celebrations, my Monday morning consists of crowded commuting, and to make matters even more miserable, it's raining heavily.

So much for summer being here, I think as I leave the tube station and walk to my office, trying my best not to get poked in the eye by the numerous umbrellas that are bobbing about near my head in the hands of all the other worker drones around me.

A bad-weather day in a season that should normally bring sunshine is annoying at the best of times, but when a wedding is on the horizon, it is downright troubling. Nobody wants a downpour on their big day, but getting married in England comes with no guarantees of good weather. A couple's best bet to hopefully get some sun on their wedding day is to plump for a summer wedding, but even then, it's uncertain. And today just proves that.

I'm damp and feeling as dreary as the weather outside as I make my way into the office, not to mention still a little dehydrated after my exploits in the bars and clubs of Manchester less than forty-eight hours ago. But it's nothing a quick trip to the coffee machine in the kitchen can't fix, and by the time I sit down at my desk, I am ready for work. Or at least I would be ready if I could be bothered to do some work.

But who is full of drive and motivation on a Monday morning? Not me, and not most of my colleagues either by the looks of it, and that's why, barely half an hour into the working week, most of us are spending more time procrastinating than producing.

My own personal procrastination has led me to the messages in my Instagram account again, and while I haven't had a chance to check them this morning after a hectic start to my day, I have certainly been meaning to. That's because I am hopeful there will be more messages from Tristan waiting for me when I do.

I was awake until almost 1 a.m. last night messaging him, and we only stopped when he told me he was tired and had to get some sleep before work. We said goodnight to each other and left it at that, but as I open my inbox again today, I see he has already picked up where we left off.

Good morning, Kate. I hope you aren't too sleepy today. I'm pretty tired myself but it was fun to chat. Have a good one at work.

'What's got you so happy?' comes the question from

Miranda, my colleague who sits beside me. When I look up, I see her staring at me.

'What?' I say, putting my phone down because I didn't realise anyone was watching me.

'You've got a big grin all over your face,' Miranda tells me. 'So what is it? Let me guess. Something to do with the wedding? God, you blushing brides make me sick with how happy you are all the time.'

Miranda is only joking about me making her sick because I know she is genuinely happy for me and my current relationship status. Having worked at neighbouring desks for the last four years, there was no way I wasn't going to invite her to my big day, and she accepted quickly, telling me it would give her a great opportunity to do something a little more fun on a weekend than asking her husband to turn the volume down when a football match was on the TV.

'Erm, yeah, just wedding stuff,' I say to Miranda, disguising what I was really happy about, which was, of course, Tristan's message.

I tell Miranda then about the dress I found, and she's excited for me, demanding to see a photo, but I make sure not to show her the price because she'll surely wonder how the hell I can afford such a dress when she's on a similar salary to me.

The arrival of our manager into our section of the open-plan office makes us quieten down and get on with our work then, but I still manage to send several sneaky messages to Tristan throughout the morning. He replies quickly, telling me he is bored at his desk, a fact I can relate to, and then we end up chatting about our jobs.

It's crazy that all this conversation has come from me accidentally liking one of his photos, but the longer it goes on, the more I'm beginning to wonder when it will end. If he keeps replying to me and I keep replying to him, when will it stop? And do I even want it to?

The fact that I keep smiling every time Tristan sends another message gives me my answer, and besides, it's not as if I have too many messages to field from the other man in my life. I haven't heard from Mark all day. He had already left the house and gone to work before I woke up, and he hasn't texted me at any point to either see how I am today or to apologise for having yet another go at me late last night. So I tell myself, if he isn't messaging me, why should I feel bad when somebody else is?

It's a little absurd, but I catch myself thinking how, although it's still early days, it's clear to me that Tristan is far more caring and attentive than Mark is. My evidence for this is the fact that he told me he hoped I wasn't too sleepy after our late night conversation last night. Then there are the questions about my wedding and how I'm feeling about it.

Tristan seems to genuinely care. But why? What's his end game here?

And, more importantly, *what is mine?*

It's a relief when my lunch hour arrives because I can then get away from my desk and message freely without worrying about my boss spotting me picking up my phone every five minutes. I end up spending that whole hour going back and forth with Tristan, the sandwich I picked up from a café on my way into the office sitting untouched on the table in front of me as my fingers fly across my phone's screen, constructing another response.

Tristan is so quick to reply, and the faster he gets, the faster I get, to the point where I'm wondering if either of us have got any work done today. But I guess having a desk job means it's possible to not always be working. We look busy, but that doesn't mean we are busy, or at least we are only busy working on our personal life rather than our professional one.

Having more than covered the topics of our upcoming weddings, our career choices and even touching on a few hobbies (he likes classical music and athletics, while I confess I like reading romance novels and going for weekends away in the countryside), we reach the mid-point of the afternoon, and there is still no sign of our chat slowing down. In the end, the only thing that does bring a temporary halt to it is when my manager, Claire, asks me to come into her office for a quick word.

I do as she says, wondering what this could be about, but it doesn't take long to find out.

'Look, Kate. I know you're getting married soon, and I'm sure you still have lots of things to sort out before then, but when you're here, I expect you to work,' my stern boss says from behind her desk, which is covered in dull stacks of paperwork.

'I am working,' I insist, but there's something about the way my manager is looking at me that tells me my lies aren't going to be believed in here.

'You've been on your phone all day. Every time I look at you, you're texting somebody. I don't care who it is. Your fiancé. Your bridesmaids. The vicar himself. All I want is for you to concentrate on your work while you're at work. Is that too much to ask?'

Damn it, I guess I have not done as good a job of pretending to be working as I thought. My excessive phone use today has been picked up on, and I don't have any excuse

for it. But at least Claire just thinks I've been wedding planning. Better that than her knowing the truth.

'I'm sorry, you're right. I have been a little distracted. But
it won't happen again. I'll get back to work, I promise.'

'Thank you,' Claire says. 'Let's not have this conversation
again, please.'

And with that, I hurry out of her office before she can say
anything more about my lack of professionalism today.

True to my word, I make sure to focus on the job I'm
being paid to do, and that's why I make it all the way to five
o'clock without looking at my phone again. It's not easy
though, and I hate knowing that Tristan will be wondering
why I stopped replying to him. I guess I'll just tell him the
truth about my boss catching me and telling me off. He
might laugh at that and tease me a little, and would that be
such a bad thing?

No sooner is my working day done than I am logged off
and heading for the door, saying goodbye to Miranda and a
few other colleagues on my way out. I leave the office and
step out into yet more rain. As I hurry to the station, I check
my phone to see what Tristan has sent since I've been offline,
but before I can, I notice I have a missed call from a number
I don't recognise.

Who could this be?

Is it Tristan?

No, surely not. How would he have my number?

There's only one way to find out, and that is to call it
back. As I wait for the line to connect, I am almost hoping
that it is Tristan and that he has found a way to call me,
although it would be a little unusual if he had. But of course
it's not him. Instead, I hear Chrissy's voice at the other end of
the line.

'Hi, Kate, thanks for calling me back. I was trying to get hold of you earlier to let you know that the dress you wanted to try on has come into the shop a little earlier than expected. So it's ready whenever you are.'

'Oh, that's great, thanks,' I say before wondering again if it's such a good idea to try on a dress I definitely can't afford.

'I'm not sure where you are now, but we're open until seven tonight if you wanted to come in this evening and try it on?' Chrissy offers, and I stop walking towards my station then and think about her idea.

'Tonight? Erm, yeah, I could do that,' I say, figuring it would be easier to go to the shop now while I'm already in the city.

'Great. I'll see you soon!'

I end the call and alter my course, walking away from the station and on instead to the wedding dress shop.

The place I first saw Tristan.

The place I first saw Tess and the dress she plans to wear for her wedding to him.

The place I am going to try that same dress on myself.

14

I walk into the shop excited but nervous.

I'm excited to try on the dress.

But I'm nervous about what I'm going to do next if I like it.

'Hey! Welcome back!' Chrissy says, forcing the friendly smile of a customer service assistant onto her face when she sees me enter. But she failed to do it quickly enough; I saw how bored and fed up she looked as I passed the windows to this shop just before walking through the door, and because of that, I feel an urge to not disappoint her now.

It's obvious that Chrissy doesn't particularly like this job, or maybe she even would go so far as to say she hates it, but getting a sale would surely cheer her up. She might get some commission for it, and I bet the commission on a £6,000 dress amounts to a juicy sum. But I have to remind myself that I can't just do what I feel might make other people happy. This is about me and what will make me happy, and as much as I expect I will love the dress I'm about to try on, I have to weigh up the pros and cons of whether or not I should actually commit to it.

'The dress is hanging up in changing room two if you'd like to go right in and get ready to try it on,' Chrissy says, gesturing to the small rooms at the back of the shop. 'Just take your time. And remember, there's no need to worry if the dress isn't quite the right fit. There's still time for alterations. But only just!'

I smile at Chrissy before heading to the changing rooms, trying not to let her hint at how soon my wedding is coming around stress me out too much.

Entering changing room two, I find exactly what Chrissy promised me. As I inspect the garment hanging against the wall in front of me, I realise I am screwed now. Just seeing this dress up close convinces me that I'll never find a more beautiful garment to wear for my wedding day than this one. Running a hand over the sumptuous fabric, I visualise myself wearing it. I won't have to imagine for long because I can actually try it on with Chrissy's assistance just as soon as I've taken my clothes off.

Getting undressed, I try to conceive of any imaginable scenario that involves me being able to pay for this dress, but by the time I'm in my underwear, the best plan I have come up with involves robbing a bank before fleeing to Mexico straight after the wedding, so that's hardly ideal.

But that's not going to prevent me from finding out what this dress looks like when it's on my body, so, together with Chrissy, I carefully slip into it, feeling the softness of the material on my skin as I fill it out and allow her to adjust certain parts slightly before taking a deep breath and looking up at the mirror in front of me.

That's when I get my first glimpse of what I could look like on my wedding day.

And that's when I know I'm really screwed.

As I suspected and hoped, but also somewhat feared, I look incredible in this dress. No wonder Tess went for it; it would be hard for anybody to look bad in this extraordinary thing. Already I'm imagining everybody's expression when they see me coming down the aisle. The turning heads, the intakes of breath, the quiet whispers of admiration. If I'm going to have all eyes on me, then this is the only thing I want to be seen in, and the more I stare at my reflection, the more I feel like I never want to take this dress off ever again.

But I have another compulsion too.

I have a compulsion to let Tristan see me in this.

Because if he did, would he be tempted to go for me over the other woman who also plans to wear this dress?

'How are you feeling?'

Chrissy's voice from the other side of the changing room curtain snaps me out of my daydream as I realise that she's left me on my own in here. I realise, too, that I'm not walking down the aisle but still in the shop, which reminds me just how far I still have to go to make my fantasy a reality.

'How's the dress? Do you like it?'

'I love it!' I say, just being honest. But will I be honest when it comes to discussing whether or not I can afford to order it?

'Fantastic! Come out so we can have a proper look?'

Chrissy is inviting me to pull back the curtain and let her see me in the dress, and I guess it's her way of offering her professional opinion and being supportive. But I'm nervous. I'm nervous about her telling me she loves it too because that will make it even harder to retreat from this dangerous situation.

But I do look good, so wouldn't it be nice to have somebody else confirm that?

'Okay,' I say before taking a deep breath and revealing myself to the shop assistant.

The squeal of joy that immediately greets me when the curtain is pulled back tells me everything I need to know about what Chrissy thinks.

'Oh, my goodness! You really do look amazing!' Chrissy tells me, clapping her hands together in excitement. I guess this must be the part of the job she enjoys, and maybe it makes up for all the long, boring hours when she has little to do but wait for another customer. Whatever it is, Chrissy is certainly happy now.

'You think it suits me?' I ask, still being a little coy but needing one more assurance.

'Are you kidding? That dress looks like it was made for you!'

I thank Chrissy whilst also wondering how many customers she has said that to in her time working here. Does she really love it as much as she is saying, or does she just want the sale? Am I a real person to her or another transaction? Perhaps there is a clue when Chrissy speaks again.

'It's up to you whatever you do, of course, but if you would like to take the dress, then it would just be a £500 deposit today, and the rest would be payable at the final fitting, though we have a few options we can discuss around that.'

'Oh, okay,' I say, being brought horribly back down to earth by the mention of money.

Chrissy seems to realise that because she speaks again quickly.

'But that's just if you'd like to pay for the dress all at once. There are payment plans that we offer, and we can discuss those too – if that is something that appeals?'

I nod mutely, and she continues her sales patter.

'We appreciate that our brides have lots of outgoings at a time like this, so we do try to make things easier where we can. There are twelve- or even twenty-four-month payment plans available, if either of those would be more suitable for you.'

It's a relief that Chrissy wouldn't expect me to hand over £6,000 for the dress today, or indeed anytime soon, and a two-year payment plan does sound a whole lot more manageable. But it's still the same amount of money leaving my account, just over a longer period.

I look down at the dress, smoothing it over my waist and hips.

Should I say no? *Can* I say no?

'Would you like me to take any photos of you in it?' Chrissy suddenly asks. 'So you could have a look when you get home and give it a little more thought?'

'Oh, erm, okay, yes, please. Thank you.'

I grab my phone from the pocket of my jeans, which lie discarded on the floor, and hand it to Chrissy. She gestures to a low circular podium, and I stand on it, slightly stunned, as she starts snapping away, capturing my image from an array of different angles.

'It's good to see what other people will see,' Chrissy says as she hands my phone back to me, and I look through all the photos. As I do, it's impossible not to fall in love with the dress even more.

'I think we have a winner,' Chrissy says when she sees the smile on my face. 'Your fiancé is a very lucky man. Sorry, what was his name again?'

'Tristan,' I reply without even thinking, before realising my mistake. 'Oh, I mean Mark.'

Chrissy looks confused, but I laugh it off and make a joke. 'Sorry, I meant Mark. I've been watching a TV show, and the main character's name is stuck in my head.'

'Must be quite the main character if you're getting him confused with your fiancé,' Chrissy says with a wink before she tells me to take as long as I need with the dress and that she'll help me out of it just as soon as I'm ready.

I stand on the podium for a few more moments, reluctant to take off the dress and put on my boring, mundane clothes again. But then I have to return to reality and find myself walking away from the changing room with a strong sense of trepidation. Every step I take towards the desk where Chrissy is now sitting causes me to imagine all the digital numbers pouring out of my bank account and into the account of this wedding dress business. Chrissy's boss will surely be delighted when she finds out that they haven't sold just one of the most expensive dresses here recently but two.

'So what do you think? Are you going to say yes to the dress?' Chrissy asks me, jovially referring to the popular TV show that bears the name of that catchy question.

This is my chance. My opportunity to walk away. To save myself the stress of finding a way to pay all that money, which is way over the budget I allocated for my wedding dress. And perhaps, even more importantly, to put a stop to this silly notion I have of Tristan seeing me in the dress and somehow choosing me over Tess, saving me from a lifetime of potential misery with Mark.

Say no, thank Chrissy for her time and then walk out the door without looking back.

'Yes,' I say, almost giggling with excitement as I do. 'I'll take the dress.'

'Amazing!' Chrissy claps her hands and rushes over to give me a hug, possibly just happy to see me find a dress I love. Or maybe it's because she knows that a hug at a moment like this helps reassure the customer that they are doing the right thing and that the staff in this shop have a heart and aren't just interested in extracting the maximum amount of money from their customers' bank accounts.

'Okay, congratulations!' Chrissy smiles warmly at me. 'Now let's get down to business because if I remember rightly, your wedding date is not far away,' she adds, professional again now as she takes a seat at her desk and invites me to do the same. 'We can discuss any alterations you might want shortly, but, first, let's get the necessary admin out of the way. Kate, how would you like to pay for the dress?'

I feel like answering that by saying I'd like to wake up now and realise that all of this was just a nice dream but that it's not realistic, just like most of my dreams aren't either.

Chrissy wants an answer.

Chrissy wants my money.

'The twenty-four-month payment plan, please,' I reply quietly, feeling like that's my safest option but still not wanting to work out exactly how much that will require me to pay each month by way of a direct debit.

'No problem! We will still require the £500 deposit up front, but after that, on this payment plan, it will be £229 a month for the next twenty-four months. Is that okay for you, Kate?'

Is that okay? Despite spreading it out over the next two years, that figure is almost as much as I pay towards the mortgage on my house. Is it too late to back out? Chrissy would be so disappointed if I did, but then again, she's not the one committing to spending all this money, is she?

I am.

I'm the one who will be burdened with the debt.

Why did I have to see Tristan and Tess in here? Why did I have to find out which dress she went for? And why did I have to start messaging him and fantasising about him being the man I would marry instead of Mark?

That chain of events has led to me saying what might just be the dumbest thing I've ever said in my life.

'That's fine, Chrissy. I can give you my bank details now.'

15

I make my way home with my bank account five hundred pounds lighter and my mind heavy with confusing thoughts of what I am actually doing with my life. I'm marrying a man I'm not sure I love or if he loves me. I'm messaging another man who I am attracted to, but, like me, he is already taken. And last but not least, I've just bought a dress I can't afford all because I saw someone else buy it before me and I decided I wanted to look as good as her.

Envy. Regret. Uncertainty. Lust. Naivety.

Fantasy.

All the above have conspired to land me in this unorthodox situation right here.

I arrive home just after seven o'clock, far later than I normally would do, but I have good reason for that, and when Mark asks me where I have been, I tell him.

'My dress was ready to try on,' I say with a smile. 'And guess what? It was perfect, so I've ordered it.'

'Great,' Mark says, completely nonplussed by my news. 'What's for dinner?'

'Excuse me?'

'I asked what's for dinner? I had a look in the fridge when I got in but can't see much in there to make a meal with. I thought you might have been at the supermarket tonight, not trying on dresses.'

Is he serious?

'I found the dress I am going to wear when I marry you!' I cry, suddenly incensed. 'Couldn't you at least pretend to be interested and forget about your damn stomach for one minute?'

'I'm not going to apologise for coming home from a hard day's work hungry, only to find my partner is nowhere to be seen and the fridge is empty. Great, you've found a dress for the wedding, but that's one day. But me coming home from work and finding my partner missing is not something I want to become a habit.'

'A habit? I was trying on a dress so I will look good for you when you see me walk down the aisle as your bride. What part of that don't you understand?'

'I don't have time for this. I'll go to the supermarket myself.'

Mark storms past me to grab his coat from the hook, and while I feel like stopping him, if only to argue some more, I realise it's best to just let him leave. Sure, it might be partly my fault there is no food in the house, and it's true that I was going to pick a few things up on the way home, but then I got distracted with the dress situation. But if he's going to talk to me like this, then I'd rather he leave and give us both a break, and that's exactly what happens after he's slammed the door and disappeared out into the night.

Alone and angry, I slump down onto the sofa and waste five more minutes worrying about what I am doing with my life. But I'm sick to death of feeling sad when it comes to men, and that's when I remember that there is one man in my life at present who offers an antidote to my unhappiness. Taking out my phone, I open the chain of messages that Tristan and I have been exchanging recently, and I decide it's time to initiate another conversation.

Finally found my dress today! Confession time – I was inspired by the dress I saw your fiancée looking at, so I tried it on myself and I loved it! So I guess I owe her a thank you, not that I'll ever see her, I suppose.

I send the message and wonder what Tristan will say back. It's not as if I've got much else to occupy myself with, and I'd rather think about him than what Mark's mood might be like when he gets back from the supermarket.

A beep heralds the arrival of a new message.

Congratulations! And wow, I didn't realise you were going for the same dress as my fiancée.

That's all Tristan says, and now I worry that I shouldn't have confessed to copying his partner's choice of dress, so I send another quick message to justify it a little.

Thank you. I really struggled to find the right dress. Believe me, I tried on almost every one in London! Ha!

A joke should go some way to making this seem less

weird, I think, and it does the trick because Tristan sends back a laughing face emoji before another message.

I can see why you chose it. It is beautiful. I'm sure you'll look great in it. Prepare to turn heads! Your partner must be looking forward to seeing you in it!

Reading that Tristan assumes I'll look great in the dress and will turn heads does wonders for my confidence, but what if he's just saying that to be nice. I mean, he hasn't seen me in the dress, has he, so how could he know for sure? Then there's the part about him assuming my fiancé would give a damn about my dress and what I look like in it.

I don't think Mark does.

But maybe Tristan is different.

Typing out the words on my phone before I chicken out, I take a deep breath and press send. As I wait for Tristan's reply, I stare at the risky statement I have just put to him.

I told my fiancé I'd found the perfect dress, but he wasn't bothered.

What will Tristan say to that admission?

Oh no, that's a shame. I'm sure he cares, really. I guess it's hard for a guy to get excited about a dress though!

I smile at the message because Tristan is just trying to cheer me up.

Thanks, but he should at least pretend, right? I mean, you went dress shopping with your fiancée. That shows

you care. My partner doesn't give a damn. Sometimes I
wonder if he really wants to marry me at all.

I'm so angry at Mark right now that I don't mind talking about him negatively with somebody else. In my mind, this only serves him right for the way he behaves towards me. I also don't mind being so honest about my fears. I know I'm escalating things, but what have I got to lose?

I'm sorry to hear that. I'm sure your fiancé loves you.

I write back.

I'm not so convinced.

Oh no, really? Wish there was a way I could cheer
you up.

I stare at what Tristan has just written. He wishes he could cheer me up. What does that mean? Is he just being nice, or is there more to it?

Thank you. You're so kind. But don't worry, I'll survive.

I message him back just as I hear the front door open, and Mark bursts back into the house.

'Forgot my damn wallet!' he cries as he storms past, barely glancing at me on the sofa.

I decide it might be best to stay quiet, so I say nothing as I listen to him stomping around, and write another message to Tristan instead.

*I might have found the perfect dress. But what good is it
if the man I bought it for doesn't care to see me in it?*

At first glance, it would appear that I'm referring to Mark, but secretly and just as easily, I could also be referring to Tristan. The fact that I'm not quite sure who I was referring to makes me even more anxious as I wait to see what Tristan's reply will say.

*Like I said, I'm sure you'll turn heads in it. I might not
have seen you in the dress, but I know you'll look
amazing.*

His words make me smile, and armed with the knowledge that I have several photos on my phone that Chrissy took of me in the dress, I offer an invite to my new buddy.

*You could see me in the dress if you like. I have some
photos from when I tried it on. But no pressure! Just a
thought!*

I wait for Tristan's reply while listening to Mark still stomping around the house, looking for his wallet. I wish he'd just find it and leave again because his presence is really distracting me from talking to Tristan and only adding to my nervousness as I wait to see if he will take me up on my offer.

Yeah, sure! Send me a few photos over!

Tristan wants to see me in the dress. This is just so exhilarating that it's only now I realise for sure that I really chose it for his benefit, not Mark's.

*Thanks. I'll send you a few pictures now. This will be a
big help. I just need your honest opinion if it's the right
dress for me or not.*

I only say that to try to justify why I'm sending another
man photos of myself in a somewhat sexy dress as I go into
my camera roll and search for the best images to send him.
I'm being slow and deliberate, careful not to send him any in
which I might have my eyes closed or just not look quite as
good as I could. But Chrissy took lots, and I'm grateful for
that because it means I have a few really nice ones that I can
feel confident show me in my best light.

Okay, here they are. Go easy on me!

I send him three photos, one of me standing directly in
front of the camera with my full body on display, one from
the side in which I look quite slim, but it must just be the
angle, and the third, which is more of a close-up that just
shows my face, neck and the top half of the dress.

What will he think? Will he like the photos? Will he
approve of the dress?

Will he think I look sexy in it?

I'm so interested in what Tristan might say when he
replies that I have failed to notice that I'm no longer alone in
the room. I only realise it when Mark steps towards the sofa.

'Who are you texting?' he asks, startling me and almost
causing me to drop my phone, though I just about manage
to keep hold of it.

'What? No one,' I say, wondering if Mark was standing in
the doorway when I was smiling widely at Tristan telling me
he would be happy to see my photos.

'I called to you from the kitchen a moment ago, but you ignored me,' Mark says, looking and sounding angry. 'Here I am trying to find my wallet so I can go out and buy us some food, and you're more interested in your phone than talking to me.'

'No, I'm not. I'm sorry.'

I close down the messages before Tristan has a chance to react to the photos, and I begrudgingly accept that I'll have to wait until Mark has left again before I check for his response. But Mark isn't going anywhere at the moment.

'You're always on your damn phone,' he almost shouts. 'Is it too much to ask that you put it down and help me?'

'No, of course not, I'm sorry,' I reply, trying to appease my partner because I'm afraid that if Mark suspects something, he might be about to ask to see what I've just been doing.

'It's not good enough. I'm tired and hungry, and you're just sitting here on that bloody thing! Who are you messaging?'

'Just the girls.'

'Let me see!'

Before I can stop him, Mark reaches out and swipes my phone from my hand.

'Hey!' I cry, leaping up off the sofa to try to get it back before he can check my messages. But he holds it out of my reach as he runs from the room, and I give chase, desperate to stop him seeing Tristan's name.

'What are you hiding from me?' Mark cries as I follow him into the kitchen.

'Nothing! Just give it back!'

But it's too late.

'Who the fuck is Tristan?'

'What?'

I try to play dumb, but then Mark turns the screen towards me. It's locked, which is a relief because it means Mark doesn't actually have access to all my messages. But he can see the new notification that has just arrived, which tells me I have a new message on Instagram from Tristan.

'Who is this guy, and why has he just sent you a message?'

'What? I don't know!'

'Are you cheating on me?'

'No, of course not!'

'If you are, then, Kate, I swear to God I'll kill you! I mean it! I'd never be able to forgive you!'

At that moment I fear Mark might hit me. He raises his hand with my phone in it, and he looks like he might bring it down on my head.

It's been all psychological abuse so far, but what if it's about to turn physical?

But Mark doesn't hit me, though what he chooses to do instead is not much better. He throws my phone at the wall as hard as he can, and it makes an awful cracking sound when it hits. Then he storms out of the room, telling me that he is going out for dinner and won't be back until later. As the front door slams, I think about going after him to try to calm him down.

But then I think about Tristan too and how I have no idea what his reply says.

That's why I forget about rushing to the door and simply rush over to my phone instead.

16

I t's the day after my heated exchange with Mark, an exchange that not only resulted in him accusing me of cheating on him but also resulted in him breaking my mobile phone. I don't want to risk logging into my Instagram account on our shared home laptop, so that means it's been impossible for me to see how Tristan responded to the photos of my dress.

But I'm hoping it's not going to be impossible for me to find out today.

I've had to wait until my lunch hour to go to the mobile phone repair shop on the high street near my office, but I'm here now, and as I enter, I am quickly met by a customer service assistant in a bright yellow shirt.

'Hi and welcome to Phixing Phones. How can I help you today?'

The overeager man – who's called 'Ricky' according to his name badge – waits for my answer, no doubt hoping I'm going to tell him that I want the latest phone to hit the market, the one that costs over £1,000 and does all sort of things that the older models can't. But I don't ask to see any expensive devices just yet, nor do I want to see them if I can help it. I just reach into my handbag and take out my older, somewhat decrepit device instead.

'I dropped my phone yesterday, and it's not been working properly since,' I say, showing Ricky the damage.

He takes it and inspects the cracked screen and the massive chip on the left-hand side before frowning.

'Dropping did all this damage? Where did you drop it from? The top of the Empire State Building?'

Ricky clearly fancies himself as a little bit of a comedian, but I don't have time for jokes.

'Can you fix it?' I ask, praying that it's a simple yes and I can have a fully functioning phone again by the time my lunch hour is over. Since it got thrown against the wall, I've not been able to access anything on there. I can't make calls, read messages, or even go on the internet because the screen is so damaged that it's impossible to see what I'm doing. No wonder Ricky suspects that I'm lying when I said I dropped it, but I'm hardly going to tell him my fiancé broke it in a fit of rage.

'I'm not a miracle worker,' he tells me as he continues to inspect the useless phone. 'But give me a minute, and I'll see what I can do. In the meantime, have a browse of some of the phones we have for sale here. Just in case it's bad news and you need a new one.'

Ricky walks away then, and I watch him go and sit down beside some guy who couldn't look more like a technology engineer if he tried. The two of them then have a good look at my phone, carefully taking it apart and examining its interior. While they do that, I take Ricky's advice and have a browse of the phones on display, but I'm quickly put off when I see the price tags next to them.

I really hope I don't have to buy a new phone because that will be another substantial outlay that I can ill afford to commit to. The knowledge that my first direct debit payment on the dress is due in a few weeks means I need to save every penny I can now, so I stop shopping around and make my way over to the desk where the two experts are at work.

'Sorry to rush you, but I really have to get back to the office soon,' I say. 'Is my phone fixable?'

Ricky shares a glance with the man beside him, and he shrugs before answering me.

'You'll need a new screen, but the SIM card is not damaged, so it'll still work. The only thing I can't fix is the big chip on the side.'

'That's fine. I don't care about that. I just want to be able to make calls and read my messages again.'

'No worries. Give me half an hour, and I'll have it sorted for you.'

I thank Ricky and the man beside him, a man who must have to deal with people's broken phones every day yet still retain some measure of enthusiasm about his job.

I decide to go for a walk to kill the time it will take for my phone to be fixed, opting to get away from Ricky and the expensive devices that surround him and enjoy a little bit of fresh air instead. But my mind is full of questions as I head out the door, and all of them relate to Tristan and that unread message of his that's residing on my stricken phone.

What does he think of me in the dress? Does he like it? Does he think I look beautiful? Or ugly and fat? What if he laughed? What if he makes me feel foolish for getting my hopes up and sending him the photos in the first place?

They're all paranoid but somewhat valid concerns, but I won't have any answers until my phone is back in my hand and I can read that latest message of his. But while that message and what it might contain sparks excitement in me, it was also the cause of my argument with Mark, an argument that at this moment has still not been discussed or resolved.

After breaking my phone, Mark stormed out of the house, and he didn't return until almost eleven o'clock. When he did, he said very little as he got into bed beside me, even as I again told him that I was not cheating on him and that he'd overreacted. The only thing he did say was that he loved me and didn't want to lose me, words that he uttered quietly before rolling over and closing his eyes. I didn't say anything after that, but I did spend plenty of the night doing a little soul-searching because, while I am not technically cheating on Mark, he was right in that I was messaging another man, and I have to accept that would trouble him. I also have to accept that I was not paying much attention to him when he was trying to find his wallet to go out and buy us some food, food that was not in the house because I had been too busy thinking about the dress and Tristan.

I have to accept some blame for what happened, though I still believe Mark overreacted and was not justified in making such a violent show of emotion as to throw my phone at the wall. But I've not said sorry yet, and neither has he, which means tonight promises to be just as awkward when we're together again at home later.

But one problem at a time.

Thirty minutes passes by slowly, but it's finally up, and as I walk back into the shop, Ricky is already expecting me.

'Here's your phone. Good as new. Well, almost.'

I take it from him and see that it now has a new, crack-free screen. There is still the damage on the side of the device, but I can live with that. I just want it to work, and after pressing a couple of the buttons, I see that it does.

'Thank you. How much do I owe you?' I ask, but my mind is more focused on scrolling to Tristan's message than reaching for my purse.

'Sixty pounds.'

'Really? That much?'

I let out a sigh before taking out my credit card and wincing slightly as I see it getting another expensive work-out. That's sixty pounds that could have gone towards my wedding dress, but now it's gone on fixing my phone. But at least it's now back in action, and no sooner have I left the shop than I open my Instagram messages.

The latest one is from Mark. I see he has sent me a funny video of two cats on a swing in a park followed by a heart emoji, his way of apologising for last night's events because he knows I like cats. But I ignore that and go to the message I really care about, which is the one Tristan sent me yesterday.

Bracing myself for his thoughts on me and my dress, I open it. But it seems I had absolutely nothing to worry about because the man whose opinion matters way more than it should has given his seal of approval in an emphatic way.

Wow, stunning! You look fantastic! The dress really is beautiful, but I guess it requires a beautiful lady to carry it off...

I couldn't have hoped for Tristan's reaction to be any better than that. The words he has used are amazing.

Stunning.

Fantastic.

Beautiful.

I'm beaming as I stare at my screen, but my smile fades a little when I realise how long ago his message was sent.

Seventeen hours. Damn, that's a long time for me to have not replied to him.

Not wanting to waste another minute, I quickly write a response.

Thank you so much! Sorry for the late reply! I had phone troubles, but it's fixed now!

I think about sending the message as it is written, but just before I do, I wonder what might happen if I was to tell the truth. What Mark did to my phone was out of order, but he felt he had a good reason to do such a thing. He was jealous. Should I tell Tristan and see what he thinks of that? The possibility excites me; it's a way of raising the stakes just a little more.

Deleting everything but the first sentence, I decide to write something slightly different to Tristan, something a little riskier and more revealing, but something I am very interested to see how he responds to.

My partner caught me texting you and got jealous. I told him nothing was going on, but he got so angry that he threw my phone at the wall! Maybe it is my fault...

I deliberately write that last part to see how Tristan reacts. Will he take my side or have some sympathy with Mark? It doesn't take long for me to find out.

*Hey, I wondered what had happened to you! I was
starting to worry! Sorry to hear about what happened
with your partner, that sucks. But I guess my fiancée
might be jealous too if she knew I was messaging
someone else so much. Maybe we should stop. What do
you think?*

I like the first part of his message because it shows he
was missing me and thinking about me. But I don't like the
last part because I really don't want these messages to end.

I don't know. What do you think?

I send back, turning the question on him.

If he suggests we stop, then I guess I'll have to go along
with that. But I really hope he doesn't. Right now, his
messages are all I have to look forward to.

I think we should stop.

He says in response, and my heart sinks as I read those
few words. I guess this is it, then. It's over, whatever *it* was.
But then he sends me another message straight after
that one.

*But only because I think we should do something else. I
think we should meet up. What do you say?*

17

Tristan wants to meet me in person. I can't believe it. That's both an exciting and a daunting invitation, and it's one that poses a couple of important questions.

Why?

And should I say yes?

They are the questions that have been on my mind all afternoon as I've sat at my desk and tried to figure out the right thing to do. My first instinct was to agree because I'd love to see Tristan for real, in the flesh, rather than forever communicating through our phones. But I paused before accepting the invite because I must think of Mark and what it might mean for my relationship with him if I was to go and meet another man.

If Mark was so jealous of me texting another guy, so angry that he broke my phone, I'm scared to imagine what his reaction might be if he finds out I'm meeting that guy. And what about Tess? She'd be jealous too, and could I blame her?

But despite those concerns, I tell myself that the fact is that Tristan and I are just friends. Our relationship is purely platonic. We've done nothing to feel guilty about, or at least nothing beyond a couple of messages that contained a few compliments that could be construed as very mild flirting. But perhaps the only reason we've not done anything more yet is because there's only so much we can do over the phone.

But that might all change when we are in the same place as one another.

While it was fairly easy to keep things sensible on Instagram, all bets could be off when we meet up, and that's the thrilling but dangerous thing about it all. Anything could happen when we're physically together, especially if alcohol is involved, and while I never had myself down as a cheat before, I've also never been seriously tempted before either. But I'd sure be tempted if Tristan was to make a move on me at our meeting, and who is to say that he wouldn't?

What would I do if he kissed me?

Run home to Mark?

Or kiss him back?

The butterflies I can feel fluttering in my stomach suggest I already know the answer, which is why I haven't replied yet. But I need to. I can't just leave Tristan hanging again, so I send him another message after sneaking away into the office toilets so my manager won't see me and give me another awkward telling-off.

We could meet up, I guess. But why?

I hope my reply doesn't come across as rude, but I have

to know. There must be a reason Tristan suggested such a thing. So what is it?

I just like talking to you and, believe it or not, you're helping me with all the pre-wedding anxiety. Call me selfish, but I could do with unburdening myself a little more, so if you're free for a chat in person, I'd appreciate it.

Tristan's justification for a meet-up makes sense, although I am a little disappointed that he seems to see me as a way to stay calm about his upcoming wedding rather than for any other reason. But that's better than nothing, and it has the benefit of not adding to whatever guilty conscience I already have, so I write back.

Where do you want to meet?

My well-considered question exists for a couple of reasons. One, I haven't committed to saying yes yet, and two, learning what kind of place Tristan wants to meet me will tell me a lot about what he might hope to get from such a meeting. There is a big difference between wanting to meet in a busy park at lunchtime or wanting to meet in a quiet wine bar at night, and as such, I need to find out a location before committing to anything. But now it's Tristan's turn to leave me hanging, and after replying quickly to all my previous messages, he takes his time coming back with an answer to this particular one.

I wonder if he is just busy at work or whether this is a tactical move on his part. If I look at it from his point of view, he's had to put up with me taking hours to reply in some cases, so he might be returning the favour or simply making sure he doesn't appear too keen. Or maybe he wants my imagination to run wild as I consider all the possible places we could meet.

I'm into the last hour of my working day when Tristan eventually responds, and when he does, I find out exactly what kind of meet-up he has in mind.

There's a pub near the dress shop called the Carter Arms. Do you know it?

Of course I know it. It's where I followed Tristan to the first time I saw him. But I'll keep that part to myself.

So this is not a lunchtime meet-up in the park. This is a setting where alcohol will be present. But what harm can one drink do? And do I feel like I'm glad about that?

That sounds good. When do you want to meet?

My manager passes by my desk at that moment, so I have to hastily hide my phone under a pile of paperwork by my keyboard, but by the time I pick it back up again, I see Tristan's reply.

How about after work tonight? I could be there at half-five? That okay?

Tristan wants to meet tonight? That's much sooner than I expected. Can I do it at such short notice? And should I?

Caring less about the fact that I should probably go home and smooth things out with Mark and more about the fact that I might not have enough make-up with me to improve my appearance, I debate my decision before deciding that I daren't turn down Tristan's offer in case he never suggests it again. This might be the one chance I have to meet him before my wedding and, therefore, my one chance to see just where this thing that exists between us might go.

That sounds fine. I'll be there!

I've done it. I'm all in now. And Tristan seems happy about that.

Great! See you later!

With the messages at an end now the date is set, I check the time and see that I have just over an hour until I am to meet Tristan face to face. That wouldn't give me much time to get ready in normal circumstances, but, given that I'm at work, I feel like I have even less time to prepare.

I need to check on my hair and my make-up, and while there's not much I can do about my outfit now, I can at least ensure it's looking okay. But I can't do any of that until five o'clock when I can leave my desk and lock myself in the bathroom.

With nothing to do until that time other than consider the strange set of events that have led to tonight's meeting with Tristan, I reflect on it all before wondering what is next. What if the pub date with Tristan is really just two people worried about their weddings who are getting together for a friendly chat over a drink? If so, that means that while it might be fun, it will only be delaying the inevitable, which is me going home to Mark and trying to manage that relation-ship as our wedding date nears. But if my date with Tristan becomes something more, something deeper, then all bets are off.

Or, more specifically, *maybe our weddings are off.*

I can't wait to get out of work. I can't wait to get to that pub. And most of all, I can't wait to find out whether Tristan has told me the truth.

Does he just want to talk, or does he want to go further than that?

There's only one way to find out. I have to go to the meeting place. Before that, I need to give Mark an excuse as to why I'll be home late.

But based on what happened last night, *Will he believe me?*

18

I opted to take the tube rather than walk, not wanting my hair to be blown all over the place by the strong breeze outside, although taking the train carried the risk it might be hot in the carriage, and sweating would then become a problem. But it wasn't too bad, and after making it to the street where the Carter Arms was located, I was ready as I ever would be for my meeting with Tristan.

As I cross the street and check the time, I see that I am five minutes early, but that's okay. I'm not going to bother playing any silly games like trying to be fashionably late. I'll just get there as close to the meeting time as possible, and I'll assume Tristan will do the same. But as I enter the pub and look around, it seems I am the first one out of the pair of us to arrive.

Not spotting Tristan amongst the crowd of patrons already in here, I make my way over to an empty table and take a seat, deciding to wait for my companion to arrive before I order a drink because that would be more polite. Checking my watch, I see it's two minutes until half-past, so he should be here any moment now. But that allows me just enough time to look at my phone and see if Mark has replied.

Knowing I needed an excuse to be home late tonight if I wanted to meet Tristan, which I most certainly did, I decided to tell Mark that it was a colleague's birthday and we were going out for one or two drinks after work. I didn't say who it was, but if he'd pressed me for that information, then I would have just given him a name because he doesn't know anybody who works at my place anyway other than Miranda, so there wouldn't be much chance of him catching me out there. But he didn't reply at all, though he did read my message, so I'm not sure what he's thinking.

Does he believe me?

Or does he suspect something is going on with me and another man?

I hope it's not the latter, but even if it is, I console myself with the knowledge that he wouldn't be able to catch me here having a drink with Tristan. That's because, unlike many couples I know, we have never done that thing on our phone in which we enable the other person to see our location at all times. I get why such a thing could be useful, but in my case, not having such a feature enabled means I can move around London freely without worrying that Mark could pinpoint my location easily and, in this instance, come to this pub to interrupt my meeting.

And that's all it is. Just a meeting. Nothing more and nothing less.

But where is Tristan?

The door to the pub opens with a loud creak, but it's not Tristan who walks inside. It's an old man in a flat cap, and as I watch him slowly make his way to the bar and order a pint of ale, I wonder if Tristan is going to be late. He hasn't messaged me to let me know if that's the case, but he could just be on the tube, and if so, he won't have a phone signal. Knowing the tube, it's not hard to imagine that he might be stuck somewhere underground now, his train trapped at a red light and waiting for the signal to change, or maybe the train has broken down altogether. But whatever is causing the delay, I do hope it's not much longer because Mark will definitely get suspicious if I stay out too late tonight.

Ten more minutes pass by, and now I'm starting to get anxious, so I decide to order a white wine to calm my nerves. But after returning to my seat and sipping half of it, Tristan is still not here, so I decide to send him a message.

Hey. Is everything okay? Still coming to the pub?

I gulp down most of my wine while I wait for a reply, but I don't get one, and with Tristan over twenty minutes late now, I'm beginning to think I've been stood up.

Feeling very much like my shy, awkward and unconfident sixteen-year-old self did way back when I got stood up for a date with the school heartthrob Johnny Stringer, I am starting to regret allowing myself to be put in such a position. Johnny stood me up that day all those years ago because it turned out that he'd had a better offer, and now I'm wondering if the same can be said of Tristan.

Is he just playing games with me? Does he do this to other women too?

Am I completely wasting my time here?

The more I wait without getting any kind of reply from Tristan, the more I think about how, while Mark might not be the perfect guy, he's never done anything like this to me.

Sure, he has mood swings and can say some hurtful things, but he's never left me waiting somewhere for him in public and failed to show up. He's always been where he's said he'll be, and there is a comfort and safety in that. It means I can depend on him if I need to, and what more can a woman ask for from her partner than for him to be dependable?

Feeling guilty now for being here rather than being at home with a man who hasn't let me down yet, I stand up to leave and turn my back briefly to the door as I pull my coat off the back of my chair. But as I do that, I hear the door open, telling me that somebody has just come in.

Turning around, I'm not expecting to see Tristan.

But it's not the person I was expecting.

Tristan is not here to meet me.

But Tess is.

19

'Hello, Kate? What's the matter? Expecting somebody else?'

I stare at Tess as she stands in front of me beside the table where I had been expecting her fiancé to come and sit, but there is no sign of him, hence my shock. All I have is Tristan's partner, who seems to be revelling somewhat in my surprise if the smug grin on her face is anything to go by.

But what is happening here?

'What's going on?' I ask before glancing over her shoulder to see if Tristan might be following her into this pub. At the moment, the only thing I can think is that Tess found out about this planned liaison and decided to come here with Tristan to tell me to stay away. But there is no sign of him joining his partner, and Tess confirms that he will remain absent.

'Forget about him. He's not coming,' she tells me. 'But I'm here now, so how about we sit down and have a little chat?'

Tess takes the seat I'd saved for her fiancé before

gesturing to me to sit down as well, but I remain standing because I have a feeling staying here will not end well for me.

'Oh, do sit down, Kate,' Tess says with a heavy sigh. 'It'll be far easier for me to tell you all the things I have to say if we're sitting. This might take a while, after all.'

All I want to do is get out of this pub and get as far away from this woman as possible because I can only believe that she is here because she thinks I've been trying to sleep with her man. Like Mark, she must be jealous, but unlike Mark, she is being very calm about this whole thing. But the fact she seems to have been one step ahead of both me and her fiancé suggests that there is a clever and calculating woman behind that calm demeanour of hers.

'I've not done anything wrong,' I say, getting that in quickly before any more can be said.

'Sit,' Tess says, sterner this time, and while I know I could just walk out of here, I need to find out what is going on. I also figure it's better if I have this conversation here, whatever it may be about, rather than risk Tess confronting me when Mark might be around. If she's clever enough to intercept my messages to her partner and surprise me here, she might be clever enough to find out where I work or live. So with all that in mind, I sit down, and once I do, Tess starts talking.

'So I suppose you're wondering why I am here instead of Tristan,' she says as she places her hands on the table, demonstrating a very confident and imposing posture. 'After all, he was supposed to be meeting you here at half-past five, isn't that right?'

I nod my head but keep my own hands off the table

because I'm feeling a lot less confident than my partner in conversation is here.

'You must have thought he'd stood you up. Tell me, how did that make you feel?'

'I don't understand what's going on.'

'No, you don't, so I'll enlighten you,' Tess says with the self-satisfied grin of somebody who holds all the power. 'You know all those messages you've been sending to my fiancé?'

I don't say anything to that, but it makes no difference.

'That's right, I know about the messages,' Tess confirms. 'You've been quite busy, haven't you? I'm not sure how you find the time to message Tristan so much, but you managed it. I'm sure you enjoyed it because he was always messaging you back. Making you feel special, valued, important. But here's the funny part, Kate. Tristan was not the one who was messaging you. It was me. I sent all those messages. I'm the one you have been talking to.'

I'm speechless.

It was Tess this whole time?

'What's the matter? You look like you've seen a ghost,' Tess says with a chuckle. 'Oh, come on, you really didn't think a good-looking guy like Tristan would be interested in someone like you, did you?'

If I weren't so shocked right now, then I might consider reaching across this table and slapping the smile off Tess's face, but I'm far too stunned to do anything other than gawk at her with my mouth hanging wide open. It seems she has successfully and completely deceived me.

But why?

'I don't understand. Why would you do this?' I ask, eager to know even if it won't change things or make me feel any better.

'Why? I'll tell you why,' Tess says, suddenly sitting forward and making me wonder if she is going to slap me instead. 'Because I know what you were doing, and more importantly, I know what you wanted. You wanted my fiancé, didn't you? You wanted to steal him from me.'

'What? No, I didn't!'

'You can pretend all you like, but the evidence speaks for itself. The multiple messages. The photos you sent of you in your dress. The agreement to meet up.'

'But you tricked me! You asked me to meet up!'

'It was a test, Kate, and you failed it!' Tess says, the smile gone now and her expression much darker. 'I was leading you on, seeing how far you would go. A little flirting here and there, a few suggestive questions. You could have stopped at any time. You didn't have to agree to come here. You could have realised that things might have been getting a little dangerous and decided to leave it at messaging. But no, you came here because you thought you might have a chance with Tristan, didn't you? You thought you might share a few drinks, and then one thing would lead to another, and just like that, you'd have another notch on your bedpost. Well, you can forget about that, because he is one man you're not getting your claws into!'

Tess raises her voice a little too much at that point, and a few others in the pub glance over in our direction, no doubt intrigued by the last couple of sentences they've just heard. But I only notice the turning heads in my peripheral vision because I have kept my eyes on Tess the whole time as she vents her fury at me.

'What did you want? A brief fling? A one-night stand? Or a full-blown affair?' Tess asks me. 'You knew he was getting married, but you didn't care about that, so what was your end game? What were you trying to ruin my relationship for?'

'I wasn't trying to ruin anybody's relationship.'

'Oh, really? Not even your own?'

'What do you mean?'

'You're getting married too, so your behaviour suggests to me that you aren't happy with your man, so you've been seeking attention elsewhere. But that's despicable. You're willing to ruin two marriages all for what? Because you fancied some cute guy you saw in a wedding dress shop and decided to stalk him until he paid you some attention? Is that it?'

'I didn't stalk him!'

'Oh, come off it. I know what you did. I had his phone. You accidentally liked one of his old photos. I've seen it all and read it all. Nothing gets past me.'

I break off from the argument for a second to question why Tess was the one using Tristan's Instagram account instead of him.

'Why were you pretending to be him?' I ask, my sense of confusion growing stronger by the second.

'Don't you worry about that. You've got more pressing problems right now, the main one being whether or not I tell your fiancé about what you've been doing behind his back.'

'Wait, no! You can't do that!'

'Give me one good reason why not.'

'Because I haven't done anything wrong! I've never met Tristan! I haven't cheated!'

The thought of Tess telling Mark about the messages and this ill-fated meeting is a terrifying one. I already know what he's capable of when he suspects me of cheating on him.

'Give me one good reason why I shouldn't contact your partner?' Tess demands, sitting back in her chair and crossing her arms.

'I'm sorry!'

''What for?'

'For messaging your fiancé.'

'Why did you do it?'

I get the impression that the only thing Tess might reward me for here is honesty, so with that in mind, I give it to her.

'Because I'm stupid,' I say, meaning it. 'I'm stupid, and I'm confused and upset, and I don't know what to do. I'm engaged to a man who treats me badly most of the time, and I'm too scared to leave because the wedding is so close now. I saw Tristan in the shop that day, and I guess I created this idea of him being some knight in shining armour who could rescue me, who would save me and change my life for the better if only we could start talking. But it was a total accident to like his photo that night, and I didn't expect him to message me. But when he did, or when you did, I was just being polite and replying.'

'Just being polite? You expect me to believe that was your only motivation?'

'Okay, I liked the attention! Is that what you want me to say? I liked the fact that a man was paying attention to me because I wasn't getting attention at home or at least not the positive kind, anyway.'

'But you admit it was wrong to keep messaging him. It was wrong to share personal things and grow closer while your own relationship was in difficulty?'

'Yes, I admit it. It was wrong! I'm sorry!'

I lean forward so that my elbows are on the table before I

put my head in my hands and feel like I'm going to cry. But Tess tells me to sit up straight and look at her because she hasn't finished with me yet.

'You want to know why I was using Tristan's Instagram account?' she asks as I fight to keep my tears and embarrassment at bay. 'I'll tell you why. It's because Tristan, the man you seem to think is so perfect and some kind of saviour, has cheated on me before and not just once. He's done it several times. That's why I am using his account. I got the password, and I monitor it to make sure he isn't secretly messaging other women.'

'But you messaged me first!'

'Only because you liked one of Tristan's photos from six years ago. Six years! I thought that was weird, so I checked out your profile, and when I did, I recognised you from the dress shop the other day. That's how I figured you must be in a relationship yourself because only a woman who is getting married goes into a wedding dress shop. But as someone who abhors cheaters, I figured you might be just as bad as Tristan, so I put you to the test. And guess what, you failed.'

'But we haven't cheated.'

'No, but I'm sure you would have, given half the chance,' Tess says as she looks me up and down and frowns. 'Then again, you are a little frumpy for my fiancé, so maybe not.'

'Why don't you leave Tristan if you don't trust him?' I ask her, but she shuts that idea down right away.

'What I choose to do with my man is up to me. It is nobody else's business,' she says, an anger in her eyes that I recognise from somewhere.

Realising that this is obviously a sore subject, I steer the conversation away from Tristan and back onto me.

'What do you want?' I ask, wondering where all this is

going. Or is it simply that Tess tricked me into coming here so she could insult me?

'I want you to leave my fiancé alone, and that includes the very idea of him. Forget all about him because he's mine. If you don't, then I will tell your partner what you have been doing, and you'll have a far bigger problem than me.'

With that, Tess stands up and turns to leave but just before she goes, she has one more thing to say.

'Relationships are hard. They don't need people like you around making them even harder.'

Tess walks away then before I can offer any kind of retort. As I watch her stride out of the pub, I feel utterly deflated.

I've been stupid. I've been naïve. And I've been caught out.

And now I have to go home, back to Mark, and hope that he never finds out about any of this.

20

I spent the entire journey home doing two things. One, cursing myself for being tricked into messaging the wrong person, and two, deleting every single one of those messages from my phone so that there is no longer any evidence of it at all.

All this time I thought it was Tristan, and it was Tess. What a joke. I would laugh if I didn't feel like crying so much. At one point I do shed a few tears, but that only attracts the glances of several of my fellow passengers on the train, so I quickly wipe my eyes and tell myself to wait until I get home before I really start sobbing.

Home.

The place I should be looking forward to getting back to. The place where my fiancé is waiting for me. And the place where I spent so much time messaging Tristan.

Or should I say, Tristan's partner.

I've been stupid on a number of levels. Thinking that Tristan actually liked me for one. I should have known it was too good to be true. Why would a man like him, with a fiancée like his, be so interested in me? I guess I created a plausible reason in my mind, telling myself that we were just nervous souls apprehensive about our upcoming weddings, assuming that the thing we had in common was the reason we found it so easy to talk to each other. But I was just being manipulated; I was being toyed with and used as a pawn in whatever game Tess was playing to make sure her partner never cheated on her again.

Do I believe her? Is Tristan a cheat? He must be if Tess is so paranoid as to have secret access to his social media accounts. I wonder if he knows. Most likely not. But I guess he's not the perfect man I built him up to be in my mind. He's just yet another heartbreaker, and considering what he looks like, it shouldn't really come as a surprise. Men who look like him have their pick of silly women like me, and that's why Tess clearly needs to keep him on a tight leash if she wants their relationship to last.

The more I think about it, the more I feel like Tess had every right to be so angry at me. Okay, so it was bad of her to pretend to be somebody else and string me along, but she was right in what she said. I was the one who made first contact when I liked Tristan's old photo, a sure sign that I was stalking him online. No doubt about it, that notification gave her cause for concern. She would have wondered who I was and started wondering if I was some old lover of her partner's or somebody new on the scene, hoping to get closer to her man.

And she was right.

I guess I was hoping to get closer to Tristan.

But in reality, I was only getting further away.

As my train reaches my stop, I briefly consider just staying in my seat and riding this service all the way to the end of the line. It's a stupid notion, but with how I'm feeling, I just want to go somewhere else, somewhere new, a place where nobody knows who I am. I feel shame and disgust, and while the earth did not open up and swallow me as I was sitting at that table in the pub with Tess, maybe if I stay on this train long enough, then I can just fall off some cliff at the end of the world and never have to face my miserable excuse for a life ever again.

But, as is the way with most people who have moments of existential dread and regret during a commute home, I do nothing at all to change my situation and instead wearily carry along on my way, walking home to my front door, where life is always the same and most likely always will be until the day that I die.

As I enter my house, once again far later than I should have been back, I vow to completely focus on my own wedding now and not somebody else's, refusing to ever get myself into such a mess as this again. It's time to forget about Tristan, or at least the idea of Tristan that I clung onto, and put all my energy into making things better with the one man, the only man, who has ever really been interested in me.

Mark.

The man who is coming towards me now with a glass of wine in one hand and an angry expression on his face.

'Oh, so you decided to come home, then. Thank you for gracing our humble abode with your presence!'

It's immediately obvious that the wine in his hand is not the first glass he's had tonight, just like it's obvious that he is mad at me. But I don't have the energy or inclination to argue. Unsurprisingly, I feel weak and wounded, vulnerable after Tess toyed with me, so all I want is to be made to feel better here.

'I'm sorry. I came home as quick as I could. It was just one drink for a birthday,' I say. 'I missed you. Are you okay? How was your day? Have you eaten?'

I'm being needy and just want Mark to love me, or at least require me to love him. If that means making him dinner or washing his clothes or tidying this house tonight, then that's fine by me because anything that will help me take my mind off what's just happened will be a big help.

'Were you with him again?' Mark asks me, the red wine swilling in his glass as he steps backwards to get away from me when I try to give him a hug.

'What?'

'Him. The guy who messaged you the other night. Tristan, was it?'

'No! Of course not! I was out for a birthday drink with a colleague.'

'Really? That's funny because I messaged Miranda, supposedly your best work buddy, on social media to ask her what time the drinks might be finished. But guess what? She had no idea what I was talking about.'

Oh no.

'Why would you message Miranda?'

'Why do you think? Because I don't trust you! And can you blame me? I've just caught you in a lie! So where were you tonight? Tell me the truth this time!'

This night is going from bad to worse, but I can't see any way to give Mark an answer that will be acceptable to him. Usually, the best thing to do in any situation is to be honest, but this is not a usual situation.

'You were with him, weren't you?' Mark insists, his eyes

glazed but focused on me, and the angrier he gets, the more I worry he might launch that glass of wine at my head.

'No.'

'Then why lie to me?'

'I don't know.'

'Give me your phone!'

Mark reaches for my handbag, but I pull it away from him, although in hindsight, it was a bad move because it only serves to make me look even more guilty in Mark's eyes.

'I know you're hiding something!' he snarls, and as he speaks, a little wine spills from his glass, the red liquid standing out prominently on the light-coloured flooring.

'Careful!' I tell him, but Mark doesn't give a damn about the wine and just demands to see my phone again.

But is it such a bad thing if I hand it over? I deleted my whole exchange with Tristan on the way home, so there's nothing for him to see on there now.

'Fine! Have a look!' I say, taking out my phone and giving it to him. 'But I wasn't with Tristan tonight!'

It feels nice to not actually be lying about that, but I still have to wait and watch Mark check my messages, just to be sure.

'See, there's nothing there!' I say defiantly.

'You've obviously deleted them,' Mark tells me. 'And you still haven't explained why you lied to me tonight. Where were you if you weren't with work colleagues?'

I can see that Mark is not going to drop this, not that I would either if I were in his position. So I need to give him something, some story to get him off my back so we can draw a line under this once and for all.

'Okay, fine. I'll tell you,' I say as my brain goes into overdrive to produce a credible story that might get me out of trouble.

And then I have it.

'I was meeting somebody, you're right about that. But it's not what you think. It was another woman.'

'Who?'

'Her name is Teresa,' I say, telling a lie, but it's close enough to Tess to keep it simple.

'Who is she?'

'She's another woman who is getting married soon, just like me,' I tell Mark as I stare down at the puddle of wine between our feet.

'Why were you meeting her?'

'Because we're both nervous about our weddings.'

'What?'

'It's like a support group thing I found online. Anyone who is having wedding anxiety can talk to another person going through the same thing; the idea is that it might help make them feel better.'

'You're having wedding anxiety.'

'Yes,' I say, and that part is not a lie either, so it comes across very convincingly.

'You don't want to get married?'

'Of course I do. But that doesn't mean I'm not nervous about it!'

'Why didn't you tell me?'

'I don't know. I should have done. I just didn't want to worry you.'

Mark ponders the story I have given him while I wait to see if he is going to buy it. But he has one more question before he accepts anything.

'So who is Tristan? I know I saw that message the other

night, so don't try to pretend like there wasn't some guy messaging you.'

'No, you're right, there was a Tristan texting me. But he's just Teresa's partner.'

'Why was he messaging you?'

'Because I was trying to arrange a meeting with her, but she was so anxious about it that she got Tristan to set it up for her.'

'What? You expect me to believe that?'

'Yes, it's the truth!'

It couldn't be further from it, but it's such a random tale that it just might work.

'So you're not having an affair,' Mark says, and I can sense the relief washing over him.

'No! Please believe me. I'd never do such a thing!'

I rush to give him a hug, and this time he is receptive to it, and as I squeeze him, I can feel his body loosening.

He believes me.

'I just don't want to lose you,' Mark admits, and I think he might actually be crying now.

It's impossible to hate him when he is like this, although once again his unpredictable behaviour has me feeling like I'm in a washing machine and am unable to get my bearings.

I've not been real with him tonight, but is he being real with me too? Or is this just another form of manipulation, another way of him controlling me?

And that's when it hits me. A thought so shocking that I almost let out a gasp.

Everybody lies.

I believed Tess when she told me why she was using Tristan's Instagram account. I bought her story about him being a cheater and her being the paranoid partner who had to keep tabs on him. And I felt shame when she told me that I had to stay away from their relationship because she knew I would bring nothing but trouble.

But what if she was lying to me? What if her whole story was concocted?

And if so, what if Tristan is in the same situation as me?

What if his partner is as bad as mine?

Or what if she's even worse?

21

Having spent the last few days mulling over my theory about Tristan and Tess and feeling desperate to put it to the test, I now have my opportunity to do just that. It's Saturday, and I've told Mark that I'm going back to the wedding dress shop to check on a few alterations. But rather begrudgingly, I've told him yet another lie.

That's because I'm not going anywhere near the dress shop today.

I'm going to that house again instead.

I've taken the car and left Mark at home, although it wasn't as simple as me just picking up the keys and walking out the front door. Mark, under the assumption that I'm a highly anxious bride-to-be, offered to come with me today, presuming that I might need his support in order to keep myself calm and not get too worked up about things. But I managed to negate his concerns and told him that I'll be fine and won't be too long, and thank heavens for that, because if he had insisted on coming with me, then I could never have driven to Tristan and Tess's place now.

Remembering the address and the route the taxi driver took to get there when he dropped me off the last time I was here, I find the street in question and park up a safe distance away from the house. Then I approach on foot, just like I did last time, and once I'm back in my fairly well-concealed spot behind the willow tree, I study the windows of the house for any sign of movement.

But I don't see anything, and with no car on the driveway, I wonder if the occupants are out. It is a Saturday morning, so it's possible they were up early and left to go and do something with their weekend. Shopping. Meeting friends. More wedding planning. Or maybe they've gone away for the whole weekend, booking themselves into a little holiday cottage for one or two days away.

The thought that me coming here might have been a complete waste of time is not a pleasant one, and I worry that I've told Mark yet another lie for nothing. But then I hear a car approaching, and as I look down to the end of the street, I see a vehicle coming towards me.

Squeezing myself up against the trunk of the tree and hiding as best I can beneath the leaves that hang down around me, I stay out of view of the driver, and it's a good job I do because once they're closer, I see who is behind the wheel.

It's Tess.

And Tristan is sitting right beside her in the passenger seat.

The car parks on the driveway, and both occupants of the vehicle take their time getting out. The doors remain closed for several moments before finally the driver's side door opens first, and Tess appears. But as soon as I see her more clearly, it's obvious that she is in a bad mood. Her face is scrunched into a scowl, and her shoulders look stiff, as if she's carrying a lot of tension in her body.

But some of that tension seems to get released when she starts shouting at Tristan.

I can't hear what she is saying from where I am, but her voice is raised, and no sooner has Tristan emerged from the car than Tess is jabbing a finger at him and continuing her tirade.

I really wish I knew what she is saying, but I daren't get any closer to the house while the occupants are both outside it, so I stay where I am and keep watch. As I do, I see Tristan put out his hands in front of himself as if to pacify Tess's anger, but it doesn't seem to do the job because her posture does not relax.

She's verbally laying into him about something, and it goes on for a good minute or so before she eventually slams her car door and walks to the house.

Tristan follows her, but as I watch him walk, he doesn't move the same way he did when I saw him in the dress shop. He looked okay there, but here, he looks on edge, timid even, and as he follows his partner inside and the door closes, I'd go as far as to say that he looked like he didn't even want to go in there.

With both of them in the house now, I don't have to worry about them seeing me so easily. But that also means I can no longer see them, so before I've given it too much sensible thought, I approach the house, sneaking down the driveway and going around the side of the property.

I don't know what my exact plan is, but I do know that I want to see the couple again and see if I can glean any more information from them without them knowing I'm watching, so I keep low as I move around the house, ducking below any windows until I reach the back of the property. When I get there, I see a larger window, and a quick look inside reveals it to be the kitchen.

It's a spacious room with a modern design, all marble worktops, state-of-the-art cooking equipment and several expensive-looking pans hanging on hooks; it's the kind of kitchen that it would be a pleasure to cook in. But it's also now the kitchen that is the backdrop to what looks like a raging argument between the two homeowners.

I keep low in the corner of the window as Tess and Tristan enter the kitchen, and no sooner have they done so than Tess turns to him and jabs her finger into his chest, causing him to move backwards a little. Again, I can't hear what she is saying, but her mouth is moving, and she looks to be straining as she talks.

But Tristan fires back with a response of his own, seemingly shouting to be heard over his partner, and the pair of them are squared off with each other as they argue right in each other's faces.

I really wish the window were open so I could hear what was being said, but it's not, so I stay where I am and make do with what I can discern from this situation. And what I can is that neither one of the people inside is backing down.

Tess turns away for a brief moment, but as Tristan tries to get her to face him again, she spins around and slaps him hard across the face.

He looks startled as he puts his hand to his cheek, but Tess does not look at all remorseful. She just walks over to one of the countertops, where she picks up the kettle, takes off the lid and then fills it up with water from the tap.

Is she really just going to make a cup of tea after striking her fiancé?

It sure seems that way because once the kettle is back in place and starting to boil, Tess takes out two cups from the cupboard before dropping a tea bag into each of them. Meanwhile, Tristan remains standing behind her, his hand still held against his left cheek.

The argument seems to have simmered down until Tess turns back to Tristan and says something to him again. Her anger seems to be building once more, but Tristan doesn't appear to be doing anything to stoke it, instead putting his hands out in front of himself again in an apparent attempt to calm her down.

But it's not working, and when Tristan goes to walk out of the room, Tess rushes after him, grabbing him and pulling him back.

What the hell is she doing? And what on earth could they be fighting about?

As I watch Tess pull on Tristan's arm while he tries to break free of her, I consider interrupting this disagreement, if only to stop things getting even worse between the two of them. But I know that to do so would give away my position, and I can't be caught here, in the back garden of somebody else's house. Tess would call the police if she saw me, and there would be no way I could justify any of this to Mark when he came to get me at the station. That's why I stay where I am for now, quiet and still, observing this negative behaviour like some morbid voyeur who is taking pleasure in witnessing other people's pain. Except I'm not taking any pleasure, because the more it appears like Tristan is in trouble, the more I fear my worries about his relationship with Tess are right.

It appears that he is in an abusive relationship too, just like me, except the abuse here crosses the boundary into the physical. And as if to prove that, I watch as Tess slaps Tristan one more time.

I'm amazed that he hasn't retaliated yet and done something to protect himself, even if it is just to push his partner away and create more space between them. It would be self-defence, so he'd be justified if he was to try to stop her hurting him, but so far, he has not touched her, and now Tess has returned to the counter, where she picks up the kettle.

'Please don't,' I murmur as I fear for a second that she might be about to do something terrible to Tristan with the boiling water, but despite turning to face him for a moment with the kettle in her hand, she turns back and merely uses it to pour hot water into the cups.

As she does that, Tristan takes a seat at the table, looking a million miles from the confident man I first laid eyes on in the dress shop. His head is bowed, and his shoulders are hunched, and he doesn't look up even when Tess places his cup of tea down in front of him and takes a seat opposite him at the table.

She sits back in her chair and sips her tea, now looking like everything is fine in her world and this is just an ordinary Saturday morning at home.

And the most worrying thing of all is that maybe it is.

Tess clearly has a hold over him.

I feel a sense of frustration rising inside me as I watch Tristan sitting there so passively, avoiding eye contact with her. And it's a frustration I recognise from my experiences with my own partner. I know exactly what it is like to live in constant fear of the person you should be able to trust the most, never knowing if they are going to be nice or nasty to you. Tess seemed like the perfect partner when she was with Tristan in the shop, but, just like Mark, she clearly has another side to her behind closed doors.

I feel like I should leave and am just about to when I see Tess bang on the table, forcing Tristan to look up at her. Once he has, she is saying something to him again, leaning forward at the table to project her point more strongly. But Tristan has clearly heard enough. He gets up to leave, but I have a feeling Tess isn't going to make it easy for him. Sure enough, I'm right. She reaches out for his cup of tea and throws it at him, the hot liquid inside splashing across his T-shirt before the cup falls to the floor and shatters.

Oh my God, this is awful.

I have to make it stop.

Looking around, I see a small stone by my feet and pick it up. Then, after taking a few steps back from the window, I hurl the stone at the glass, knowing it won't be big enough to break through, but it will sure be big enough to make a loud noise when it hits.

It does just that, and once the stone has made impact, I set off running, making sure I'm well out of the way before Tess goes to the window to investigate. But while she does, I'm hoping that should buy Tristan enough time to get out of the kitchen and go and find some peace and privacy some-where else in the house.

If he's anything like me, he might lock himself in the bathroom and have a cry.

And if there's one thing I have learned from today's visit, Tristan is much more like me than I realised.

22

I was on my way back to my car when I heard a commotion behind me, and after ducking back behind the trusty tree that has always kept me so well hidden before, I watched Tristan leaving his house while Tess called after him to come back.

Wearing a different T-shirt to the one that had tea thrown all over it only a few moments ago, Tristan seems to be ignoring his partner as he unlocks his car and gets inside, and even when Tess tries to open the door and block his way out, he just starts the engine and puts the vehicle in motion.

It's obvious Tristan is upset about what just happened in the house and wants to get away, but Tess clearly doesn't want to allow that to happen, though she doesn't stand much chance as she tries and fails to stop the moving vehicle.

Quickly reversing off his driveway, Tristan ignores his fiancée's pleas to come back and instead drives away down the street, leaving Tess standing on the pavement not far at all from where I am hiding, watching him go and no doubt wondering if she might have pushed him away.

I can't blame Tristan if he has had enough of her after what I saw her doing to him in their kitchen, but there's no way of knowing for sure where he is going and what he might do next.

Unless I follow him.

As Tess goes back into her house, I make the decision to get to my car as quickly as I can so I can try to catch up to Tristan. I know he turned left out of this street, and he can't have got far yet, so I put my foot down and head off in pursuit.

Turning left and pushing my vehicle to the boundaries of the speed limit on this particular road, I fear that Tristan might have made another couple of manoeuvres down any one of the streets that branch off from this road, and if he has, then I'll never be able to find him again. But then I see his car stopped at the red light up ahead, so I move in behind him, and when it turns green, I continue to tail him.

I have no idea where he might be going as I follow him through this suburban part of the city. The police station to report his violent fiancée? A family member or friends for support? Or a hotel so he can check in and have a night away from his crazy partner? I'm not going to lose sight of him again until I have found out, but after five more minutes of driving, I get my answer, and it's an unexpectedly simple one.

He's going to the supermarket.

Tristan turns off the main road and enters the large car park outside a popular grocery store chain, so I do the same and find an empty parking spot a safe distance away from the driver I have followed in here.

Getting out of my car, I see Tristan heading inside the supermarket, so I do the same, and as the automatic doors slide open and I step into the cool, air-conditioned building that is crammed full of shelves stocked with all sorts of food and drink, I pick up a basket to make it look like I'm just another customer. But of course I'm not. I'm not here to do any shopping; I'm here to try to talk to the man who was just physically assaulted by his partner.

Spotting Tristan at the opposite end of the vegetable aisle, I consider how he looks remarkably normal for a guy who has just come from a bitter domestic dispute. No one would know from looking at him that he's just been slapped several times and had a hot drink thrown at him. Sure, he looks a little sad and is moving like he doesn't really want to be here, but then again, he looks no different to every other man who sets foot inside a supermarket. But there are no obvious signs that this is a victim of abuse, and even though his left cheek looks a little red, it's doubtful anyone would assume it's because he's been slapped. But just because it's not obvious, it doesn't mean he's any less of a victim, and as I trail him through the aisles, watching him putting various items into his basket, I feel a bond with this man.

But I'm well aware that I previously felt I already had a bond with him only for that to blow up spectacularly in my face, so I have to proceed with caution because if there's one thing I have learnt about the couple I saw in the dress shop, it is to expect the unexpected.

I do want to make contact with Tristan though, proper contact this time, rather than online, where things can be murky and deception is much easier to hide, so I slowly get closer to him, moving nearer as he stands and inspects a row of soft drinks in the middle of the store.

Searching for some way to initiate conversation without it being obvious that I've followed him here from his house, I stand beside him and pick up a bottle of lemonade before checking the label.

'You know, I promised myself I'd stop drinking fizzy drinks this year,' I say, not looking at Tristan when I talk, but I'm guessing he'll know I'm speaking to him because we're the only two people on the aisle.

'I'm sorry?' he says, hearing me but unsure if I was actually talking to him.

'Sorry. I was just thinking out loud,' I say, and I turn to look at Tristan then, allowing him to see me in full profile because I'm curious as to whether he will recognise me or not. He might remember me from the dress shop, or maybe he saw one of the many messages I sent him on Instagram if Tess slipped up for a moment. But he isn't looking at me like somebody who knows who I am, and after offering me the briefest of smiles to be polite, he steps away to move on.

'Wait,' I say, realising that playing it slow isn't going to get me anywhere here.

'Sorry. Do I know you?' Tristan asks me, his slight smile fading as my eyes land on his left cheek.

'Yes. I mean no. You don't. But I know you. Well, kind of. It's complicated.'

I'm doing a terrible job of explaining myself, and Tristan's frown is evidence of that, so I need to sharpen up or he's going to walk away from me, and I can hardly chase him around this store, can I?

'What's going on?' he asks, his basket of goods hanging by his side.

'My name is Kate, and I know who you are. You're Tristan, right?'

'How do you know my name?'

'It's a long story, but I just want you to know that I am a friend, and I want to help you.'

'What the hell are you talking about?'

He looks around him then as if expecting someone to come and explain to him what is really going on here. Or maybe he is looking for the camera crew that might be recording this bizarre interaction for some reality TV show.

'I know what your fiancée is like. Tess. I know how she treats you. I saw her hit you.'

'Excuse me?'

'It's okay, I'm not going to tell anybody. I just want you to know that you don't have to put up with it. You don't have to marry her.'

'How the hell do you know I'm getting married? Have you been following me?'

'No. I mean sort of. But I can explain.'

'Seriously, what the hell do you want?' Tristan says as he starts to back away from me, possibly viewing me as some random, unhinged woman. Unfortunately, I do feel a little that way as I stand before him and try to explain myself.

'I saw you in the wedding dress shop.. It's a long story, but I found you online, and we were messaging.'

'We were messaging? I don't even know you!'

'That's the thing! It wasn't you who was sending me those messages. It was Tess. She was pretending to be you, and she got me to meet her, but I thought I was going to meet you. Then she told me to stay away from you.'

'When did all this happen?'

'This week.'

Tristan, quite rightly, looks like he has absolutely no idea what I am talking about, but I push on regardless because I've already committed now.

'I didn't stay away, though. I found where you lived, and I was at your house earlier when you came home. I saw Tess slap you, several times in fact. And I saw her throw the cup of tea at you.'

'How the hell did you see that?'

'I was in your garden.'

I wince as the words leave my mouth because I know they aren't going to sound good. But it is the truth, not that such a thing seems to be getting me anywhere at the moment.

'I need to get out of here,' Tristan says, suddenly dropping his basket. 'And you need to leave me alone.'

He turns and walks away then, and it's obvious that I have freaked him out with my story, but I can't let him go home without getting him to keep this little meeting from his partner, so I drop my own basket and almost run after him.

'Tristan! Please, can we talk for a minute?' I call after him as I follow him through the supermarket, but he doesn't turn back and just keeps heading for the doors, and a moment later, we're out in the car park again.

I see him take out his car key, and realise that I'm only a few seconds away from watching him drive away, so I run around in front of him and get myself between him and his vehicle. Then I put my hands out in front of me to show that I mean him no harm, much like he did when he was arguing with Tess earlier.

My sudden movement does the job of slowing him down. He stops for a moment, and when he does, I seize my opportunity to talk to him again.

'I know what it's like,' I say, slightly out of breath but not letting that distract me from the important message I need to convey. 'I'm in a toxic relationship too. I'm due to marry my partner soon, but he mistreats me. Not physically like Tess. It's more psychological with Mark. But it's still abuse.'

'Why are you telling me this?' Tristan asks before glancing around the car park nervously to see if anyone can overhear us.

'Because I want you to know that you're not alone,' I say, finding some inner strength, because I know that I'm not alone now too. 'And I want to help you.'

'Help me? I don't need any help.'

Tristan makes another move for his car, but I put my hands out and stop him. This time I touch his chest, and when I do, I notice him flinch.

'I'm sorry. I didn't mean to touch you,' I say, afraid I've just triggered him. 'I just want to be a friend and talk.'

'I don't want to talk,' Tristan says, stepping forward again. 'And I don't need a friend. I'm sorry if you do, but I can't help you. Now, get out of my way and leave me alone.'

Tristan barges past me, opens his car door and gets in behind the wheel.

I realise I've lost him now, but just before he can close his door, I have one more thing to say.

'Don't tell Tess about this!' I say, afraid she will find out I approached her fiancé and then make a similar approach of her own to mine.

But Tristan says nothing. He just slams his door shut, starts the engine and then speeds out of his parking spot, exiting the car park and leaving me standing alone in the middle of it, wondering if I might have just made a very big mistake.

23

Whenever there have been times when I've felt at my lowest ebb, then there's only ever been one thing I've done or, rather, one person I've turned to. Molly, my best friend, and the person who has always been there for me far longer than Mark or my other friends. That's why she is the one I am thinking about reaching out to now as I sit at home and dwell on my ill-fated talk with Tristan and the fact that, for both of us, it seems that abusive partners are the only ones who can win.

As I give Molly a call, I hope she will pick up, but I always know it's not guaranteed with how busy her life is. There's a good chance she's changing a nappy at the moment, or trying to put some food into a child's mouth, so she won't answer if that is the case. It's not uncommon for Molly to not return calls or even text messages for hours, though I know by now that she's not being rude, she's just drowning in a sea of responsibilities. But I'll always try her anyway, although on this occasion, once again, there is no answer.

Not to be deterred, I send her a message, hoping she'll see it soon and call me straight back.

> Hey. Hope you're okay. I was just wondering if you were free for a chat? Could do with getting a few things off my chest and feel like you're the one I want to talk to about everything. Call me when you're free. Love ya xx

I send the text and then wait impatiently with my phone in my hand to see what Molly will do. It takes almost an hour for a reply to come through.

> Hey! Sorry, just at A&E with Archie. He fell over in the garden. Is everything okay? Not sure how long I'll be here xx

It often takes a simple reminder that other people are having problems of their own to snap a person out of their personal pity party, and as soon as I learn that Molly's oldest son is in hospital, then I stop worrying about myself so much.

> Oh no! I hope he's okay! Don't worry about me, I'm fine. Just look after Archie. Send him my love xx

I feel guilty now for letting Molly know that I am worrying about something when she already has enough worries on her plate, but as always, she handles it well.

> He'll be fine. Just want to get him checked. How about I come to yours tomorrow? We could have a proper chat then? xx

I smile because while it does mean I'll have to wait

another day to get those few things off my chest with Molly, talking face to face is always better than doing it over the phone.

> That sounds great. See you tomorrow. But only if Archie is okay! Let me know how he is xx

I have no problem delaying my talk with Molly while she takes care of her son. But delaying it is all I will do because I'm still going to go ahead and talk to her about certain things, which are things that I have not shared with another person before. I'm not exactly sure how I am going to do it yet without making it seem too obvious, but I am at least going to broach the subject of abuse with my best friend and get her thoughts on what a woman should do if she was in such a relationship.

I'll just have to make sure it's not completely obvious that I'm talking about myself.

I'll also have to make sure that Mark is not here when Molly calls around.

He's at the gym now, hence why I was hoping to have a quick phone chat with Molly today, but now that she's visiting tomorrow, I'll need him out of the way then too, lest he overhears and realises I might be close to revealing his true nature to another person. Then I remember that he mentioned going to the pub with a friend tomorrow afternoon to watch the Sunday afternoon football match, so that will be the ideal time for Molly to be here.

I wait until Mark is home before double-checking with him that he is still out tomorrow, and he confirms that he is. But when he asks me what I plan to do with my Sunday afternoon, I tell him I'll just relax and maybe read a few articles about wedding things. He also asks me how I got on at the dress shop, so I must lie there as well and say everything was fine, but at least my secret trip to Tess and Tristan's place remains just that.

A secret.

The next portion of the weekend passes without incident, and Mark is in one of his good moods on Saturday night, snuggling up to me on the sofa as we watch a movie, and being light and jovial as we scoff snacks and sip wine. But he's back to his moody self on Sunday morning, which I'm almost relieved about in a way because it reaffirms my decision to talk about some of the difficult things I plan to discuss with Molly when she is here later.

Thankfully, Archie is absolutely fine after the scare he gave his mother yesterday, so Molly is able to come and see me, and as Mark gets ready to go and meet his friend at the pub, I look forward to the coast being clear with him out of the way.

'Have fun. Enjoy the match!' I call out as he leaves before quickly going to make myself look a little more presentable for Molly's arrival. She appears thirty minutes later, and after welcoming her in and making her a cup of tea, we chat briefly about Archie and the drama he caused yesterday before I gently broach the subject I've been wanting to get to all this time.

'Can I ask you something?' I say as we sit on opposite sofas with our hands wrapped around our hot drinks.

'Sure. Is it about the wedding?'

'No, not quite.'

Molly looks intrigued now, probably because I've talked about nothing but the wedding for the last several months, so this is a change of pace for me.

'I've got a friend at work who has got a bit of a problem,' I begin, keeping it vague. 'It's a relationship problem.'

'Oh, go on. Give me the gossip,' Molly says, getting even more comfortable in her seat and no doubt wondering if I'm going to give her some sordid story about an affair or some other kind of illicit scandal that she doesn't get to experience beyond watching TV dramas.

'Well, she's got this boyfriend that she's been with a while,' I say, really hoping that I'm not making it too obvious that I'm talking about myself. 'And she thought he was the one, right? She figured they'd get married and have kids and all that stuff.'

'Okay.'

'But now she's worried that she's making a mistake being with him.'

'Why?'

'He's changed since they first got together. He has bad mood swings.'

'Has he hit her?' Molly asks, cutting straight to the chase.

'No, nothing like that!'

'Good, because if he has, then she must leave him immediately. No excuses. No second chances.'

Molly looks deadly serious, and I agree with her sentiment whilst also feeling glad that she doesn't seem to have figured out who I'm referring to here.

'No, this is more psychological abuse, I suppose. One minute he's mean to her, the next he's nice. She never knows where she stands with him. But when he is mean, it's often for no good reason.'

'That's just as bad,' Molly quickly replies. 'Just because he's not hitting her, it doesn't mean he's not harming her.'

'Yeah, I suppose.'

'How is all this making her feel?' Molly asks, imploring me to delve deeper into this tricky subject.

'Erm, I don't know. Sad, I guess. Confused. Mostly just unsure whether she should leave him, but then if she does that, she'll feel like she's wasted all that time, and starting again is scary, you know?'

'Sure, but staying with him would be far worse. Better to end it now and make a clean break rather than endure it anymore. You say they're not married yet?'

'No, not yet.'

'Thank God. That's good. She can just leave him, then. It'll be far easier now than having to get a divorce and heaven forbid trying to split once they have kids. Then it'll be really complicated and messy if she wants to end it.'

Molly isn't saying anything that I hadn't thought myself, but just hearing how clear and confident her opinion is on this subject is proof that it shouldn't be quite the dilemma I'd built it up to be in my mind. I know deep down that I should not be marrying Mark, and even though I've let things get this far, even to the point of ordering a wedding dress, it's not too late to turn back.

But there is still the issue that has been holding me back the most, and it's one I want to get Molly's thoughts on before I move on to an easier topic of conversation.

'The thing is, my friend is a little on the older side,' I say, still trying to be vague. 'So she's worried about being alone at her age, and then there's the issue of starting a family and whether or not time might be running out for her there.'

'That's a shame,' Molly says, looking genuinely sad. 'How old is she?'

I know I can't give my exact age, so I decide to add a year on to this fictional character.

'She's just about to turn forty,' I say, and Molly nods sympathetically.

'Okay, well, sure, it's not the ideal age to be ending a relationship, but if it's the right thing to do, and it sounds like it is, then she can't think about that. She needs to think about what's best in the long term. I get that she might be afraid of not having children, but is it really any better to stay with an abusive guy and have kids with him? Imagine all the problems that could lead to.'

'Yeah, I guess,' I say, nodding my head and looking like I'm pondering this tricky dilemma for the first time too.

'You know, there's lots of help and guidance for women in these kinds of situations these days,' Molly goes on. 'Support groups and things like that. Hell, if the abuse is that bad, she could even go to the police, and they'd make sure she was alright.'

'The police? I don't think she needs to get them involved!'

'Okay, well, maybe not. I'm just saying that if she is feeling threatened in any way, or if she's scared of making that leap and leaving him, she doesn't have to do it alone.'

'Yeah,' I say, nodding slowly before staring down into my tea.

'But I suppose the biggest issue here is, does she really want to leave him?' Molly asks. 'I mean, it's one thing knowing what the right thing to do is, but it's quite another to actually do it. At the end of the day, people have to want to help themselves, if you know what I mean.'

I nod my head but say nothing this time, and despite it not being the wisest thing to do, I just keep staring into my drink while I think this all through. But perhaps my awkward silence is the thing that gives the game away.

'Kate, are we talking about you here?' Molly asks gently, almost causing my heart to stop with how scared I feel because she has just landed on a truth I have been trying to keep secret for so long.

'What? Me? No, it's a friend at work like I said,' I reply before laughing nervously. But Molly just frowns, and I can see that she doesn't believe me.

'You've always been a bad liar, Kate.'

'I'm not lying. This isn't about me!'

'Are you sure?'

'Yes!' I cry, and maybe if I had left it there, then Molly might have had no choice but to accept it. But I couldn't.

The tears that filled my eyes made sure of that.

All it took then was Molly rushing over to my sofa and sitting down beside me before I stopped pretending completely and accepted that my secret was now very much out in the open.

24

It's been ten minutes since Molly realised I was the woman in my story and, therefore, the woman who longs to leave the man she is supposed to marry soon. But despite that shock, my best friend has not been judgemental or even made a big deal about things, probably because she knows a huge fuss is the last thing I need at this time. Instead, she has just sat patiently beside me and let me cry onto her shoulder until I have finally lifted my head up, dried my eyes and then made it clear that I'm ready to start talking again.

'I'm so sorry,' Molly says, looking absolutely devastated for me. 'I had no idea. I thought you were happy. God, what kind of friend am I for not seeing this?'

'It's not your fault!' I say, making that very clear. 'I guess I was just good at covering it up. How were you to know? I didn't tell a single person.'

'But we talk almost every day. I should have noticed you were worried about something.'

'Molly, please. Don't blame yourself. It's not your fault.'

'Just as long as you know it's not your fault either?'

Molly eyes me sceptically then, clearly wanting to see that I am aware that I am not to blame for feeling stuck in a difficult relationship.

'Yes, I know,' I say quietly. 'It's just so hard.'

Molly wants to know the full story then, what happened, how this all came to be. So I give it to her, running through the full extent of my time with Mark, giving her all the facts, not just the ones that make him and me look good like I used to share openly in the past. I give Molly all the gory details: the mood swings, the constant fear of putting a foot wrong, the unpredictability of living with a man like Mark who seems so perfect to everybody else but only because he reserves all his imperfections for me.

'The pig,' Molly says when I've finished, pure venom in her voice. 'How could he be so two-faced? He was always so nice whenever I saw him. But all this time, he's been treating you like this. You swear he's never laid a finger on you?'

'No, definitely not,' I tell her, although I am neglecting to mention the part where he got so angry the other day that he threw my phone against the wall. That incident does suggest there is a worrying progression to Mark's moods, and who knows, maybe it is only a matter of time until he hurts me physically.

Thinking about that reminds me of Tristan and what his partner is doing to him, and I wonder if I should mention any of that to Molly now that I've already shared plenty of other things with her today. But before I can make a decision on that, Molly speaks again.

'Do you want to leave him today? Because you can. I'll help you pack your things now, and then you can come and stay at mine for as long as you need to. It'll be a bit of a tight squeeze with the kids, but we'll manage.'

The speed with which Molly seems to want me to act is daunting, and while I have now come to the grim realisation that I have to leave Mark, I don't know if I can do it that quickly.

'Whoa, slow down. I need to think about this,' I say.

'Then again, this is your house as much as his,' Molly reminds me. 'So why should you have to leave? He should be the one to move out, right?'

'I'm not sure he'd agree to that.'

Molly calms down a little bit then when she realises exactly why this isn't so simple.

'You're worried about what he might do if you tell him you're leaving him?' she asks, and I nod my head.

'I mean, I don't know what he'll say. I'm sure he'll be upset, but he might accept it. Then again, he might not.'

'Okay, well, one thing is for sure. You can't be alone with him when you tell him. You need somebody with you. Or you need to do it in a public place. You need to make sure he can't hurt you when you tell him.'

'I don't think he will.'

'But you don't know for sure, so you can't take the risk.'

Molly is making sense, as she often does, and sense coming from another person is just what I needed to hear because it's far too easy to overcomplicate things when it's all just internal dialogue running through a tired, confused mind.

'You are going to leave him, right?' Molly insists, seeking clarification because I've gone quiet again.

'Yes, of course! I just need to find the right time.'

'The sooner the better, I'd say. Not just because the

wedding is approaching but because it's the safest thing for you to do.'

Molly is right, yet again, and I don't think there's a single bit of advice she has given me that I can query or refute. She knows what I must do, and most importantly, I know what I must do.

But that doesn't mean it's simple.

'I'm scared,' I confess, although I realise I'm probably stating the obvious because Molly doesn't look surprised by my admission at all.

'That's perfectly understandable,' she says, putting her arm around me and offering a supportive smile. 'But you're not in this alone. I'm with you, and all your other friends will be too.'

'Oh God, what are the girls going to say? I've just made them spend hundreds of pounds on my hen party in Manchester, and now there's not even going to be a wedding.'

'They're not going to care about the money! They'll just want you to be happy.'

Once again, Molly is doing a great job of quashing all my fears and reasons for not just leaving Mark already, so much so that it's got to the point where I'm not sure what else I can say.

'So when are you going to do it?' Molly asks. 'You know, you don't even have to do it in person. You could just send him a text saying that you're leaving.'

That does sound easy, certainly much easier than telling him face to face. But it doesn't feel right to leave my fiancé via text. That feels like a coward's way out, and I don't want to feel like a coward in this situation.

'I think I will tell him in person,' I say.

'Okay, when?'

'This week.'

'Why not today?'

'I'm not ready.'

'Kate...'

'No, I am definitely going to do it. I just need a little more time to process things. I wasn't even planning on telling you about any of this today. You just guessed.'

'Sorry, but you made it so obvious for me!'

We share a laugh then, and it helps break the tension in the room.

'I will do it this week,' I say, trying to sound confident but also aware that what I've just said shows I'm stalling a little.

'How about tomorrow after work? I can come here to be with you.'

'Fine, tomorrow.'

'Okay, I'll see you then. Six o'clock. But only if you're sure you're not in any danger in the meantime?'

'Absolutely. Mark has never hurt me, not physically anyway.'

'It only takes one time.'

'Molly, I'm fine, honestly.'

With that, Molly lets it drop, and I thank her for all her help and support before suggesting she leave so I can have some time alone before Mark gets back from the pub. I need to calm down, dry my eyes and make it look like I haven't just spent half of the afternoon having a very deep, serious conversation about a terrible subject that involves my fiancé when I was supposed to be on my own relaxing. Mark will know for sure that something is wrong if he comes home and finds me in distress, so a little alone time will do me good.

I give Molly a big hug in the hallway before seeing her out of the front door, and once she's gone, I think about how crazy it was that I ended up telling her everything. But I guess there was part of me, some subconscious part, that wanted her to know, which was probably why my fictitious story about a work friend was so blatant that she saw through it in an instant.

But I can't regret it happening now, because this feels like a truly momentous moment for me, a real turning point. I've accepted that I'm not going to be some unhappy woman in an awful marriage. I am going to do something to change things. I am going to tackle this problem head-on.

Just not yet.

I've had enough life-altering conversations for one day. Besides, it's not just my problems that are on my mind at present.

Tristan is still a concern for me too.

I wish there were some way I could help him like Molly has offered to help me.

But how can I help him if he refuses to help himself?

25

I t's approaching lunchtime on what has turned out to be a rather busy Monday for me at work, and because of how much I've had to do since I got into the office this morning, I've not had too much time to think about my many problems.

I still haven't officially left Mark yet, but it's been less than twenty-four hours since my conversation with Molly, and despite her texting me regularly since and asking me if I was okay, I haven't told Mark that I've confided in someone else or that we have to separate. I also haven't had too much time to think about Tristan and his situation with Tess, but like my first problem, I understand that just pushing it to the back of my mind does not mean it will go away. I can't ignore these things forever, because not only am I on a rapidly decreasing countdown before my wedding, but because it's not the right thing to do.

I must leave Mark so that he might be convinced to change his ways with his next partner. I also have to somehow find a way to help Tristan so that he is no longer suffering in his own way.

But first, I'm hungry and need to go and get myself a tuna sandwich from the bakery around the corner.

Striding through reception, I smile at my colleague sitting behind the desk and ask her if she would like me to pick anything up for her while I'm out. But she says no, so I have nobody to shop for but myself as I leave my office and step out onto the sun-soaked street. But I have barely taken five steps in the direction of the bakery when I look up and see who is waiting for me outside my office.

It's Tristan.

He's standing right in front of me.

'Hi,' he says, and he offers me a warm smile, one that makes him look especially dashing, although the smart suit he's wearing was already doing a good job on that front.

But before I can greet him or even smile, I nervously look around for any sign of Tristan's partner because if he is here, then maybe Tess is too, and that would be bad news.

'Don't worry, I'm alone,' Tristan tells me, clearly picking up on my anxiety, and I relax a little now I know that Tess is not in the area. But I'm still confused as to why Tristan is here, and indeed how he is here.

'How did you find me?' I ask him, and for a brief moment, I am excited by the idea that he might have followed me like I followed him before. Some people might be put off by slightly stalkerish behaviour, but not me if the circumstances are right – and being stalked by a man like Tristan are some pretty exceptional circumstances.

'Can we go somewhere for lunch?' he asks. 'I'll tell you then. There's a lot I need to say.'

I'm never going to say no to that, so I suggest the Italian place around the corner, for two main reasons. One, it's never usually that busy, so we should be able to get a table. And two, nobody from my office ever goes there because they all thought it wasn't great value for money when we tried it the first time, so I know I won't have to explain to one of my colleagues why I was having lunch with some random guy today.

It only takes a minute of walking until we are being welcomed into the restaurant, and as a waiter shows us to our table, I think about how unexpected it is to be about to sit down for a bite to eat with Tristan, the man who practically ran away from me the last time we were together.

And it's that awkward subject that is the first thing he mentions once we are seated and looking at a menu. But before we have even ordered anything to drink, Tristan gets straight to the point.

'I'm sorry about what happened in the supermarket,' he says. 'I overreacted. I guess I was so shocked and confused, as well as embarrassed about the fact that you saw what Tess did to me.'

'No, don't apologise; it's not your fault,' I say. 'I went about things all the wrong way. I never should have followed you, and I certainly shouldn't have sneaked around the back of your house and spied through the window. I'm not surprised you ran. I must have seemed like a lunatic!'

'A lunatic? No, not quite, although I'll admit it was a little odd when you first approached me. But I should have known you were only trying to help. I guess I wasn't ready to accept that help on Saturday.'

'But you are now?'

Tristan doesn't answer, and it's not just because we're interrupted by the waiter a moment later asking us what we would like to drink. I think it's because he still seems a little unsure. But the fact he has sought me out after what happened on Saturday is a good thing, and once we have ordered a large bottle of sparkling water to share, I ask him again how he was able to locate me.

'I found your LinkedIn profile online, and it listed your workplace,' Tristan says, shattering the idea that he has been stalking me, at least in person anyway. 'I got your name from my Instagram account, or rather, my Instagram account that my fiancé has been controlling.'

'You've seen the messages I sent you?'

'Yes, and I've seen what Tess was sending back. I'm sorry.'

'But how did you see them? I would have thought she would have changed your password?'

'She did, right after she had made me delete the app from my phone last year, but she was signed into my account on her mobile. I'd stopped using social media a while ago, really; every post that went online as me was actually posted by Tess. She controlled all my accounts. But after what you told me on Saturday, I realised she was doing far more than simply sharing a few photos of me every now and again to keep up appearances. She was messaging people and pretending to be me.'

'But I still don't understand how you saw it if she changed your password?'

'She might have changed my password, but the original email that I set up the account with still belonged to me. All I had to do was click the "forgot my password" link, and that let me create a new one. Tess couldn't stop me doing that.'

I can see that Tristan seems pleased with himself about seemingly having found a way to regain access to his Instagram account. But the very fact that he would even have to do such a thing after his partner took such control over him speaks volumes about the state of his relationship. I sense that there is still very much an air of sadness hanging over this man.

'Okay, so you understand why I was concerned about you,' I say. 'After Tess met me and told me to stay away, I was worried. That's why I was at your house. I'm sorry for prying, but I was concerned, and after what I saw, it seems I was right to be.'

Tristan nods, showing me that he holds no issue with me and anything I've done so far.

'I get it. What Tess did to you, the whole pretending-to-be-me thing, asking to meet you and then threatening you. That's not right.'

'Never mind that. I saw her slap you and throw a hot drink at you!' I exclaim, holding his gaze steady as I state as clearly as I can, 'You need to get away from her, and you need to do it now.'

This is the first time Tristan doesn't look so sure. He's a full-grown, fairly athletic man, but just like I noticed on Saturday, his confidence has been destroyed, which obviously makes the decision to leave his abusive partner much harder to make.

'You can't marry her,' I tell him or, rather, I urge him. 'What she is doing to you is wrong. It's criminal, Tristan.'

'I know that,' Tristan admits before taking a nervous gulp of his water. 'It's just difficult.'

'How so?'

'Well, put yourself in my shoes. How do you think people would take it if I told them I was getting physically abused by my fiancée, a woman half my size and a woman who, to everybody else, appears to be the dream catch? I mean, how do I tell my family and friends?'

'You're embarrassed?' I ask as gently as I can.

'Yes, of course I am! I'm an adult. I should be able to look after myself.'

'This isn't your fault. You shouldn't have to deal with something like this, from anybody, never mind someone you love. She's abused your trust and taken advantage of your loyalty, and she'll continue to do so as long as you let her get away with it.'

As I say this, I'm well aware that my words could just as easily apply to me and Mark, and that's when I realise my situation might be able to make his a little easier.

'You know, you're not the only one going through something like this,' I say, taking a deep breath before I enlighten Tristan about the kinds of things my fiancé has done and how his behaviour has made me feel.

He's as shocked to learn that I'm stuck in a bad relationship just as much as I was shocked to see him waiting for me outside my office, but after that, it becomes clear that we have far more in common than our bad choices in prospective life partners.

Tristan tells me how one of the many things that has been keeping him with Tess is the fact that all his friends are married and settled down, raising families and doing what most people their age are doing, leaving Tristan feeling like he would be a failure if he wasn't to do the same. I admit that I feel exactly the same way, but then remember many of the pearls of wisdom that Molly gave me yesterday and repeat some of them here, my goal being that he needs to see sense like I have in the end.

'Don't you see how absurd it is that we're essentially so

close to doing something that will make us unhappy for the rest of our lives?' I say to Tristan once we have finally ordered our food. 'We're so close to getting married to bad people and for what? To keep up appearances? To fit in more in our social circle? It's ludicrous. Your real friends won't care if you're single or not. They just want you to be happy.'

'I know all this,' Tristan admits. 'But it's still not easy, is it? Leaving, I mean. Starting again. Being alone. Yes, all my mates will support me if I tell them, but at the end of the day, they won't be the ones going home to an empty house or having to start dating again. They've got what they need. They're already so far ahead. But I'll be back at square one, not even in the race.'

'Tristan, there is no race. The only thing that matters is that you're safe and happy. Imagine you had a son, and his partner was hitting him. What would you suggest he do? You'd tell him to leave, right?'

'Of course I would.'

'Then you should do the same.'

Tristan knows I'm right, yet he still looks like he might need a little persuading. That's when I have an idea.

'How about we make a pact?' I suggest. 'We'll leave our partners at the same time. That way we won't be alone. I'm not suggesting we get together afterwards or anything like that!' I grin, suddenly a little embarrassed about how that might sound. 'But we can support each other. What do you think? I am planning on doing it tonight, but if you're not quite ready yet, I could delay it a little. But not for too long, of course.'

I meant every part of that statement except the middle part, the part where I said I'm not suggesting that we get together afterwards, because there's no way I'm not dreaming of that somehow being the end result here when all is said and done. But there's a lot to go through before I can entertain thoughts of being with a new man, never mind one like Tristan.

We have two partners to get rid of first.

But just as a waiter emerges from the kitchen carrying two plates that I suspect are for us, Tristan has given what I have suggested sufficient thought. He has come up with an answer for me, an answer that will go on to change both of our lives dramatically in the coming days.

'Okay,' he says, looking me in the eye, an act that was hard for him to do when I first spoke to him in the supermarket. 'If you can do it, then so can I. I'll leave her.'

'Great! But you can't do it alone. It's dangerous. You'll need someone with you.'

'I could ask a friend to come to the house,' Tristan says, and I tell him that's a good idea and that I've arranged for the same thing.

'So tonight, then?' I confirm as the waiter gets closer.

'Okay,' he replies, and even though it seems incredibly scary, the pair of us know it should be done sooner rather than later. 'Let's do it.'

With that, our pact is made.

I smile at Tristan as our food gets delivered to our table, and once the waiter has left and just before we pick up our knives and forks to tuck in, I have one more suggestion to make.

'Let's swap numbers,' I say, taking out my phone. 'That way, we can text each other when we've done it. And this time, when I send you a message, I will know for sure that I'm really talking to you and not to her.'

26

Taking advantage of my manager leaving at half-past four, I managed to get out of work a little earlier than usual. After convincing Miranda to keep quiet, I left before 5 p.m. too. My reason for wanting to do so was because I was desperate to get home and make a good start on packing up my things well before 6 p.m. when Molly is due to be here, after which Mark will arrive. Then, with my friend standing beside me for support and her partner, Gary, sitting outside in the car with the kids, ready to run inside and help if need be, I will tell Mark that I am leaving him.

I'm sure he'll be shocked, most likely upset and probably angry, but it will be too late by then. I'll have a few bags full of my belongings ready to go, and Molly will make sure I get out of the front door and into her car safely. Then, once the deed is done and I'm on my way to hers, I will text Tristan and tell him the news.

At that point, I'll just have to hope that he has done the same.

Not wasting any time once I arrive home, I take out a

suitcase, the same one I used when I packed my things to go on my hen party just over a week ago, and start throwing in all the clothes I want to take with me when I leave Mark. I'm hoping that, even after I've left him, relations between us can reach a point where things are amicable enough to allow me to come back and get the rest of my stuff at another time. I have completely dismissed the idea of me staying here and making Mark be the one to move out, even though that was what Molly suggested. I understand where she is coming from, in that if Mark is the one to blame for this breakup, then he should be the one to move out, but even so, it will just be far easier if I leave. I'll be happy to walk out of the door, whereas I suspect Mark will kick up much more of a fuss, and a fuss is the last thing anyone of us needs if we are to get through this thing as painlessly as possible.

Once my suitcase is full, I leave the clothes I can't fit in there in my wardrobe and pray that they will still be intact when I return. But I can't help engaging in a little paranoia as I zip my suitcase up, visualising an angry and hell-bent Mark taking a pair of scissors to the garments I've left behind, cutting them into small pieces and taking great, sadistic pleasure in it all.

But he wouldn't do that, would he?

Pushing that scary thought from my mind, I haul my suitcase off the bed and put it by the bedroom door, where it will stay until I've spoken to Mark in Molly's presence. Putting it by the front door will only tip Mark off that something is wrong before I've had a chance to say anything, so I won't do that.

As I check the time, I see that Molly is due any minute now, and Mark should be about twenty minutes behind her, giving me and my best friend a little prep time to go over exactly what I will say and allow me to relinquish any last-minute nerves in front of her. I can't fathom how she is able to find the time to help me with a problem like this whilst juggling her own schedule, but she's my best friend for a reason; she's always there for me, no matter what. I'll have to make sure to say a big thank you and buy a suitable present for her once all this is over, so that she knows exactly what her help meant to me at this difficult time. The same goes for Gary too, because I can't imagine he was thrilled when he found out that I would be moving in with his family for a little while, but whatever grievances he might have, I know he'll put a brave face on and welcome me in just as kindly as his wife.

I move around the house, killing time, fidgeting nervously as I pick up and put down random objects. Then, in the kitchen I notice that the clock is ticking its way past six, and there is still no sign of Molly. Her presence here is designed to be calming, but her absence only heightens my anxiety as more and more minutes tick by and she still doesn't show up.

Where the hell is she?

I try her phone, ringing her three times, but there is no answer. The text I send her also goes unanswered, and as the clock hits 6:20 p.m., I know I'm almost out of time. Mark will be back any minute, but I'm so stressed by now that I know if I'm alone with him, then I can't go through with this.

Telling myself that it won't come to that, I decide to message Tristan to ask him how his own plans are going this evening. He was going to ask his best mate to come and help him deliver the message to Tess, so I have to hope that all goes to schedule there. But Tristan's reply a minute later is a very troubling one.

> I've changed my mind. I'm not going through with it.

My heart sinks. Why has Tristan backed out of what he was going to do? He seemed so certain of it at lunchtime. But, not wanting him to be deterred, I respond quickly.

> You can do this. You know it's the right thing to do. Remember what we talked about. And remember you're not alone x

I send my message as fast as I can, praying that Tristan still has his phone in his hand and hasn't completely made up his mind yet. It turns out he is still holding his phone, but what he says this time is even worse.

> No, I'm not doing it. Leave me alone. We can't talk again.

An awful realisation dawns on me, and while I can't know for sure what has happened, it seems there are only two possible options. Either Tristan is so afraid of Tess that he has come to this conclusion himself in the last few hours since we parted, or even worse, Tess has discovered what happened and has forbidden him from speaking to me ever again.

I'm so concerned about Tristan's predicament that when I hear a car outside, I automatically assume it is Molly, and I rush downstairs because I want to tell her about this man I am trying to help. But when I open the front door, I see who is actually parking up, and it is not my best friend.

It's Mark.

He is home before Molly has got here.

So what do I do now?

'Hey, what's this? Coming to greet me at the door? This is quite a homecoming!' Mark says with a big smile as he walks towards me with his briefcase in hand. 'Everything okay?'

'Erm, yeah,' I say before he leans in and gives me a kiss, but my eyes don't close, nor do they look into his as he nears me. Instead, they are looking down the street, where I am hoping to see Molly on her way here. But there's no sign of her, and after Mark has passed me and gone into the house, he asks me why I'm leaving the door open.

'Oh, I forgot to tell you. Molly is calling by,' I tell him, looking back out onto the quiet street.

'No problem. What for? Never mind, I don't need to know about girly gossip. I'll go and grab a shower and stay out of your way. Maybe when she's gone, we could order a takeaway? I know it's only Monday, but why not treat ourselves for surviving the worst day of the week?'

With that, Mark heads up the stairs, whistling as he goes, and while I should be pleased he is in such a good mood, there is something disconcerting about just how happy he is, especially when it is in such contrast to how worried and afraid I am.

I'm worried and afraid for Tristan. But the longer Molly fails to show up or even reply to my calls or messages, then I'm worried for her too.

This is not like my best friend. She would never do this at any time, but tonight, when she was supposed to be here to help me leave Mark?

Something is not right.

But what can I do? I can't stand by the open front door all night, waiting for her to show. I also can't risk leaving Mark if she is not here.

I close the door and decide to go and unpack my things while Mark is in the shower.

As I'm doing that, I hear that he is still whistling, and from where I am, it sounds as though he doesn't have a single care in the world.

27

I was able to unpack my suitcase without Mark seeing what I had done, but that didn't mean the rest of my night went smoothly. I spent the whole of it waiting to hear back from Molly, yet she made no contact with me at all. I got so worried that at 9 p.m. I messaged Gary and asked him if Molly was okay, but he hasn't replied to me either, the message remaining unread and, therefore, my worries remaining unresolved.

But I seem to be the only one with the weight of the world on my shoulders. Mark has been in a great mood ever since he got home, and as the night starts drawing to a close and we prepare to get into bed, he only seems to be getting happier.

'I've had a nice evening,' he muses as he pulls back the duvet and eases himself onto the mattress, looking very well fed after our takeaway earlier. 'I've been wondering why we can't have nights like this more often. No arguments, just a nice atmosphere in the house. Maybe some of that has been my fault. But I want you to know that I'm going to strive to make sure most nights are like this one from now on.'

It's surprising to hear Mark admit what he just has, and I'd surely be more receptive to such an admission if I were concentrating on him and not on my uncontactable best friend who was supposed to have been here three hours ago. But my mind is too clouded with thoughts of Molly, so I barely acknowledge Mark's statement and just get into bed alongside him before turning off my bedside light.

Annoyingly, he tries to initiate sex then, but I fend him off by telling him the takeaway has made me feel a little nauseous, although it's probably just because I overate rather than because the food wasn't cooked properly. But Mark seems to buy it, because he just kisses me goodnight and then rolls over, and once his bedside light is off too, I pick up my phone and check for any new messages again.

Lowering my screen brightness so that there is less chance of Mark noticing that I'm using my device instead of going to sleep, I check for any word from Molly or Gary, but there is none. I also check social media for any recent updates on either of their accounts because at least that would tell me that they are okay and have been up to something fun tonight, even if they have been ignoring me.

I'd happily take being ignored as long as I knew Molly was fine.

But I still don't know that for sure as the clock ticks past 10 p.m. and all remains quiet.

But then it happens.

At 10:20 I receive a text message from Gary, and what it says has me sitting bolt upright in bed in shock.

> Molly is at the hospital. She had a fall at
> home. The doctors are with her. I'm not
> sure if she's okay.

'Oh my God!' I exclaim as I reach for the bedside light, and once it's on, I scramble out of bed and start getting dressed.

'What's going on?' Mark mumbles as he wakes up after a very short sleep to find me rushing around the bedroom.

'Molly's at the hospital! I need to go!' I say, getting dressed in record time before rushing for the door.

'What? Slow down!' Mark calls after me as he gets out of bed too, but there's no chance of me doing that, and I'm already halfway down the stairs by the time he is on his feet.

'Wait! I'll drive you!' Mark tells me as I put on my coat and shoes, and even though I'd rather make the journey alone, I realise I'm hardly in a good state to operate a car.

I'm so shocked by this. Molly is in hospital. She's hurt. That's why she didn't come here tonight. That's why she didn't contact me. She's injured.

But how badly?

Mark rushes down the stairs to join me, and after quickly putting on his coat and shoes, we're ready to go.

He asks me about Molly and her condition as he drives me through the quiet streets towards the hospital, but I say very little to him, not only because I'm still in shock but because I know very little myself. All I have to go off is what Gary said in his text, and despite replying to tell him that I'm on my way, the only thing he has told me is which ward he is waiting in.

The lack of traffic on the roads at this time of night allows us to reach the hospital quickly, and once we've found the relevant department on the numerous signposts that are dotted all over the exterior of the building, Mark and I make it to where Gary is sitting with a few family members beside him.

'Is she going to be okay?' I ask as I give him a hug before acknowledging Molly's parents, a couple I know well, having been around them numerous times at events over the years.

'They're not sure. She banged her head,' Gary tells me, the pain and worry etched all over his face.

'What happened?' Mark asks as he puts an arm around me to offer support, a gesture that I don't actually pull away from because I could use a little reassurance, even if it is from the man I was supposed to leave four hours ago.

'I got a phone call from the school to say that Molly hadn't shown up to collect the kids this afternoon,' Gary says, the stress threatening to break him as he tries to hold himself together. 'I tried calling her but got no answer, so I went to the school and then took the kids home. But when we got there, I found Molly lying at the bottom of the stairs. She must have fallen down.'

I put my hands to my mouth, horrified at not just the accident itself but the fact that her husband and children walked in and found her like that. Those poor kids. They must have been so scared.

'She was unconscious, so an ambulance was called, and when she got here, they took her in for an operation,' Craig, Molly's father, says, picking up the telling of the story because Gary is currently too emotional to say anything more. 'They think she has bleeding on the brain.'

Edith, Molly's mother, starts weeping at that, and I decide it's best to give them all a break from my questions, so I tell them that everything is going to be okay before taking a seat with Mark a couple of rows behind them to give them a little space.

Shellshocked, but not half as much as the poor family sitting in front of me on these plastic chairs, I sit beside Mark as we wait for a doctor to come out and give us some news, praying that when it comes, it will be of the good kind and not the bad. While waiting, I hear Gary on the phone, and it sounds like he's talking to his parents, who I figure are looking after the kids at home. But other than that, very little happens for almost two more hours, other than Mark offering to go to a vending machine and pick up a few refreshments for everybody.

But then, not long after midnight, a man in a white coat walks through a set of double doors, and as he approaches, the expression on his face tells me he does not want to have the conversation he is about to initiate.

Trying to persuade myself that I'm just being paranoid and that he is actually here to deliver good news, I grit my teeth and hold my breath as I watch him ask Gary to come into another room with him. But that seems to be a suggestion that tips off both Gary and Molly's parents that something bad is coming, and after they have urged the doctor to just deliver his update right here in the waiting room, that update is eventually given.

'I'm so terribly sorry. The injury to Molly's skull was too severe for our surgeons to be able to help her. She passed away ten minutes ago.'

An awful, unnatural silence falls over the waiting room for several seconds, seconds that are characterised by a realisation that for all of us here, our lives will never quite be the same again because Molly will no longer be in them.

Then the questions start, coming from Molly's family, but none of the answers change the outcome.

That's when the crying starts.

And by the time the howls of pain are coming from Molly's mother, that's when Mark suggests we go home and give them some space so they can grieve as a family without us getting in the way.

28

The drive home from the hospital is a total blur, the glare from the bright streetlights not doing enough to snap me out of my trance and allow me to hear anything that Mark is saying beside me. The only sound I can hear is that howl of pain that Molly's mum let out after learning her daughter had died, and even though that occurred ten minutes ago, it's playing over and over again in my head.

It's the early hours of the morning by the time I get back into bed, but I'm not crawling under the duvet to sleep. Instead, I'm crying, and they are the kind of tears that come from the knowledge that I'll never see my best friend ever again.

I'm so upset that I barely hear Mark when he asks me if he can get me anything.

He's sitting on the bed beside me and stroking my hair, and I'm too weak to say or do anything, whilst wondering how I'm ever going to possess the energy to get out of this bed again now that I'm in it. I just can't comprehend that

Molly has gone forever. I only saw her yesterday. She was right here in this house, sitting on my sofa downstairs and talking to me. More than that, she had her arm around me as I cried into her shoulder after telling her about what Mark was really like, and in that moment, I felt I was closer to my best friend than ever before.

But now we couldn't be further apart.

To think I'll never be able to sit down and have a cup of tea with her ever again. No more catchups, girly chats and general gossiping, nor any wild nights out or weekends away with the rest of our friends. This chapter of my existence is over, the chapter in which I always felt that, no matter what disasters occurred in any other area of life, be it my love life or my career, there would always be one constant whom I could count on regardless.

Molly.

Good old Molly.

But now, the late Molly.

Mark is still stroking my hair as the pillow becomes increasingly damp where my face is buried into it. When I finally lift my head for a little air, Mark is on hand to give me several tissues, and after drying my eyes and blowing my nose, I have a brief moment of rest before the inevitable tears are due to start again.

'I just can't believe it,' I say. 'I can't believe she's gone and in such an awful, stupid way. Falling down the stairs. What a waste of life. Her poor kids.'

I can't imagine how Gary is going to tell his children that their mummy is not coming home, and that's when the damn tears start again, my eyes stinging with how much they hurt, though it's nothing compared to the pain inside my chest at what I've personally lost. But racking my brains for something, anything, that might give me a little comfort at this difficult time, I remember the promise I made to Molly the last time I saw her.

It was the promise that I was going to leave Mark, as she advised. Now she's gone, I'm the only one who knows about that conversation, and I feel like the right thing to do would be to honour the promise I made her and make good on my decision to leave Mark. The only problem is that I'm in no state to enact such a dramatic thing right now, not after what has happened tonight.

But one thing this awful episode has done is given me an excuse to postpone the wedding, that looming deadline that still feels like a ticking clock always operating in the background.

'We'll have to cancel the wedding,' I say to Mark as I keep sobbing.

'What? Why would we do that?'

'Molly was my chief bridesmaid. I can't get married without her.'

I think that's a perfectly valid reason, but Mark does not agree.

'Are you joking? We can't cancel. The invites have gone out, and everybody has made plans to be there. What's happened with Molly is a terrible tragedy, but she wouldn't have wanted you to not get married.'

'But I don't want to. Not yet anyway. It's too soon. How can I smile and enjoy what should be the happiest day of my life when I'll have been at my best friend's funeral only a few days before?'

I feel like my concerns are legitimate, but Mark is clearly annoyed and gets up off the bed and starts pacing around.

'Look, I'm sorry. I'll support you at this difficult time, but we are getting married as planned, and that's the end of it.'

'Mark—'

'No, you listen to me. The wedding goes ahead!'

He goes to leave the room then and mentions something about how he'll sleep downstairs tonight so that I have some space, but I'm not letting him walk out on the conversation like this. He has to listen to me. He can't just expect me to be quiet and do whatever he says.

'Mark! Stop!'

He spins around in the doorway then, but when he does, I see a different look on his face than the one he had a moment ago when he was stroking my hair in bed. This one is dark, very dark, as if there is a storm brewing behind his eyes, and just seeing that shift in his demeanour tells me not to say another word. But Mark has something else to say, and when he speaks again, what he tells me makes my crying stop, though they are as far from words of comfort as it's possible to get.

'I don't want to hear another word about cancelling or delaying the wedding, and as well as that, I don't want to hear another word about Molly,' he says. 'I don't want you up here for days crying and being of no use to me. You sort yourself out, and you get back to work. We have a wedding to prepare for, and I'll be damned if this or anything else gets in its way.'

Wow, this is a new low, even for a man like Mark, who has said some horrendous things to me in his time. But this is the winner. This is officially the worst thing to ever come out of his mouth in my presence.

'How can you say that?' I ask him, mortified. 'A poor

woman is dead, and her family are in pieces, and you are telling me to forget about it and move on? Really?'

'Yes, really,' Mark says before he takes a menacing step towards the bed, a movement that makes me afraid to say anything more. But Mark clearly has momentum now, so he doesn't shut up just yet.

'Can't you see? Being friends with that woman has done you no good. Now she's gone, you're free to be yourself and make your own decisions.'

'My own decisions? What do you mean?'

'You know exactly what I mean.'

'No, I don't! What are you talking about?'

'I'm talking about the conversation you both had in this house on Sunday while I was at the pub!'

Mark's words are like a punch to my stomach. How the hell does he know that Molly was here on Sunday? And even more so, how does he know what we talked about?

'What?' I utter, the only word I'm capable of squeezing out at this time.

'Did you really think I wouldn't find out what was going on behind my back?' Mark says, his eyes boring into me. The way he is standing over me by the bed makes me feel smaller and more vulnerable by the second. 'Did you really think that you could just leave me?'

I can't believe it. Mark knew what I was planning to do. *But how?*

'What are you talking about?' I try, but it's a lame attempt at pretending I have no idea what he's referring to, and just as I thought, Mark sees through it easily.

'Oh, come off it, Kate. Stop playing dumb because I'm far too clever to let you hide behind that ploy. I know what you talked about with Molly, and I know what the pair of you planned to do this evening.'

I don't say anything this time, allowing a silence to fall between us that Mark seems to revel in until I pluck up the courage to speak again.

'How?' is all I can ask, and that question seems to be the one Mark was hoping for.

'It's funny because I always thought that I would keep quiet and not let you in on what I did,' he says with a wicked smile. 'But where's the fun in that? So here it is, and you're going to love it when you hear it, especially the part where I tell you that you're the one who started this whole thing.'

'I started it?'

'That's right. You started it when I saw that message on your phone from somebody called Tristan. The way you were acting then, desperate for me to give me your phone back after you'd been spending so much time on it, that was what made me realise you were capable of hiding things from me. So I decided to do something about it. It's quite simple, really. I took your phone while you were sleeping, and I installed spyware on it.'

'Spyware?'

'Yes, it's technology that allowed me to see all your incoming and outgoing messages and, most importantly, who you were talking to. I did it at first because I was worried about this Tristan fellow and wanted to see if you were cheating on me. But when I saw you message Molly and tell her that you needed to get a few things off your chest, it made me wonder if I perhaps had bigger problems than you potentially cheating on me. It made me wonder if you were planning on talking about me. It made me wonder if you were going to go crying to your best friend about how you make me behave.'

I cannot fathom what I am hearing, which is why I say nothing as Mark continues.

'Being able to see your messages, I saw that you arranged for Molly to come here on Sunday, rather conveniently during the time when I would be out at the pub. The very fact you wanted to talk to her when I wasn't around only increased my belief that you were going to complain about me to her. But I couldn't know for sure, of course, not if I wasn't actually here to witness the conversation. So that's why I had to make sure I heard what the two of you discussed without being present in the room.'

My mind is racing as I try to think of all the ways Mark might have been able to eavesdrop on my and Molly's conversation. But it seems I'm way off the mark while I'm imagining him lurking outside trying to listen in through the walls.

Because then he tells me how he managed it.

'The bookcase in the living room is a great place to store things,' Mark says. 'But it was only on Sunday when I realised just how adept it is at hiding a small recording device.'

'You recorded us?'

'Just the audio,' he says, as if that is any more acceptable than recording images too. 'I just needed to hear what you were saying to Molly and, boy, did I hear it! You certainly were loose lipped, weren't you? It was kind of cute how you concocted some story about a woman at work having issues with her partner, but Molly wasn't so dumb, at least not as dumb as she looks, and she figured it out pretty easily in the end, didn't she? She knew you were talking about me. And that is why she told you to leave me, which is exactly what you were going to do when I got home from work earlier.'

I stare at Mark, trying not to give anything away with my facial expression because I don't want to confirm that everything he has just said is 100% correct. But he already knows it is, and there's no way I can deny it, so I don't even bother.

'So what were you going to do when you got home – and I left you?' I ask him, my hands holding on tightly to the duvet that covers me, as if this flimsy bit of material could protect me if he decided to suddenly attack me for daring to want to leave this awful relationship. 'What were you going to say when Molly was here, and you couldn't keep up your act of being a great guy in front of her anymore?'

I'm genuinely intrigued as to know how he was going to convince me to stay when I was standing beside Molly with my suitcase by my feet, a situation that tragically never materialised.

'Oh, Kate, come on now. Think about it,' Mark says as a dastardly sneer spreads across his face.

So I do.

I think about it.

And that's when the full horror of what might have really happened here dawns on me.

29

I'd surely have been safe to assume that my best friend dying would be the worst thing that could happen to me this year.

But it turns out there could be something much worse than that.

My fiancé might have been the one who killed her.

I had been far too stunned to speak when Mark dropped his very heavy hint about possibly having something to do with Molly's 'accident', and that was why, when he left the bedroom, I remained under the duvet, too scared to go after him or even to call out and ask him some questions. But my fear wasn't just born out of being afraid to hear Mark say anything more about what he might have done to Molly. It was also a fear that I might have been in danger myself by knowing too much.

If he has hurt my best friend, what would be stopping him from hurting me too?

Despite wanting to know more, I knew it was a huge risk to press Mark for more details, so I stayed quiet, and I stayed that way all night, including when Mark eventually came to bed and got in beside me. He seemed to be revelling in my silence, surely well aware of how nervous I must have been as I pondered the idea of him being a killer. He must have known that for me to say something would have been to put myself in danger. He must have known that I was more likely to choose the safer option, which was to say nothing at all and hope that, somehow, this might all just blow over.

I spent all night trying to tell myself that Mark did not really hurt Molly and that it was just an accident like everybody else believes it to be. She just fell down the stairs, which is a terrible thing to happen, but don't the statistics show that most accidents happen in the home? It's a place where people assume they are safe, and therefore, they don't quite pay enough attention to things, resulting in it being quite dangerous. Molly wouldn't be the first person to die from suffering a fall in her house, and she won't be the last, so it is plausible that it was an awful but innocent event.

But then the other part of my brain, the part that refused to let me sleep because it kept telling me there was another side to the story, constantly reminded me of the way Mark told me to 'think about it'. Not only that, but the sinister smile that spread across his face was like a window opening and giving me a glimpse into a dark and dangerous world, one that he was more than happy to give me a sneak peek into because he knew it would frighten me enough to never want to venture there again. Mark wanted me to know that such a side to him exists, a dangerous, possibly murderous side. Then he went back to being his normal self, as if nothing had happened, except of course it has, and neither of us can ever forget it.

The sunrise that came after a very long night was just as

painful for me as the sunset that preceded it several hours earlier, and as the light streamed in around my bedroom curtain, I thought about all the horrible things that would be happening today.

Molly's family were waking up to their first day without her, and pretty soon, all of her friends would know about her death too, joining me in this world of pain. There would be lots to do at the hospital in terms of dealing with the body before, inevitably, funeral arrangements would have to start being discussed. And then, somehow, everybody who knew Molly would have to start trying to get on with their normal daily duties, be that going to work or tidying the house or even something as simple as remembering to feed themselves. I'm expected at my office in a couple of hours, where a full day of administrative tasks await me. But how am I supposed to go and concentrate on work when I've only just begun processing my grief?

I should call in sick and ask for compassionate leave. I'm sure my manager would understand. Losing a best friend warrants a little break, surely. But just before I can pick up my phone and call somebody to let them know I won't be in today, a thought crosses my mind, one that makes me pause.

If I don't go to work, that means I have to stay here all day.

Isn't that far, far worse?

Mark is still lying beside me, presumably asleep, and even though I can't see how I can summon up the energy to get dressed and leave the house, I know I'd rather do that than stay here with him for another minute longer than I have to. I also wonder if putting a little distance between myself and him might be the thing to snap me out of my fearful state, and once I'm away from him, I might feel confident enough to possibly go to the police and tell them that they might need to treat Molly's death as suspicious rather than accidental.

Is that what needs to happen? Do I need to make the police aware of a potential problem, or will they already be looking into it themselves? Will they just blindly believe what the doctors say seems to have happened, which is that Molly had a fall and hit her head, or will they wonder if somebody might have pushed her? If so, they will want a suspect, and I could give them one of those to help them along. But will they believe me? And what evidence would there be to make Mark sweat? If he did kill Molly, then he must have been careful. A man like him, who downloads spy software on my phone and plants audio recorders in our house, is clearly always one step ahead, so he wouldn't hurt Molly unless he was sure he could get away with it. The idea of giving his name to the police only to see him get off without charge is horrifying, because then he would surely come after me and make me pay.

But what's the alternative?

Say nothing? Do nothing?

Let him get away with murder?

I need to get out of this bedroom and, ideally, out of this house, so I carefully peel back the duvet and climb out of bed, being extremely careful not to disturb Mark. Treading cautiously over the floorboards, I make it to my wardrobe and open the door ever so slowly, desperate for it not to creak. A noise like that would be practically deafening in this silence. Only after I have managed that do I start taking out a couple of items of clothing, again extremely careful about not making any sounds, well aware that something as stupidly simple as a coat hanger hitting the back of the wardrobe could cause Mark to stir and ask me where I am going.

With my clothes in hand, I creep to the bedroom door, and once I make it there, I realise I can get out of the bedroom without waking him. Moving into the hallway, my confidence grows as I increase the distance between me and Mark, and when I get to the bathroom and close the door slowly behind me, I feel like I can do this.

As I get changed quickly, I briefly check my reflection in the mirror, but I know I don't need to look perfect before I go out today. I just need to be gone before Mark wakes up. That's why, once my clothes are on, I go to leave the bathroom again, neglecting the other parts of my normal morning routine like brushing my teeth and combing my hair in favour of saving precious time.

Opening the bathroom door again, I go to step outside, aware that I'm now just one short trip down the stairs away from getting out of here, and from there, I will have a little time and space to decide what to do next. Go to the police? Go to the hospital? Go to Molly's family? Run a mile to get away as quickly as possible? All are good options that I will consider just as soon as I leave and—

'Good morning. You're up early. What's the matter? Struggle to sleep?'

The sight of Mark standing between me and the staircase is a shocking one, and I instinctively take a step backwards into the bathroom once I know he's there. He sees me do that and seems to take pleasure in it before stepping forward while noting that I am dressed and seemingly ready to go out.

'Where are you going?' he asks as I stand frigid in the bathroom doorway, debating whether to try to rush forward to get past him to the stairs or to fully commit to going back in the bathroom and locking the door behind me so he can't follow me in.

'Work,' I reply quietly.

'You're planning on going to work after what just happened? Oh, I don't think so. You've just lost your best friend. I think you need some time off.'

'No, I need to go in. There's lots to do and—'

'Don't worry about it. I already let your boss know you wouldn't be in today. She totally understands and told me to tell you that you should take as long as you need until you feel ready to go back.'

'What?'

'I messaged your manager. Claire, right?'

'When did you do that?'

'Last night while you were in bed. I could see how upset you were about Molly, so I knew there was no way you'd be fit to go into the office today.'

'How?'

'You mean how did I get her number? Oh, that was easy. That software I put on your phone, the one I mentioned last night? It allowed me access to all your contacts, and because you'd already told me her name, I found her easily enough and sent her a text telling her what had happened. She replied immediately, offering her condolences. Do you want to see her message? It really was nice. I'm not sure why you complained about her in the past; she seems a lovely person to work for.'

'You messaged Claire?'

'Yes, and she isn't expecting you today and probably not all week, if I'm honest, so don't worry about it. You can get back into bed if you like, unless you want breakfast? Can I make you something? I've told my manager what has happened, so I've got some time off as well, which means I can be here to look after you.'

This is getting worse by the second.

'Depending on how you feel, I was thinking we could perhaps do some more stuff for the wedding a little later on,' Mark continues. 'Seeing as we're both off work for the foreseeable future, we could use this time to our advantage and tidy up a few last details. Is that table plan finalised yet? What about the songs for the DJ? Did we do that already? We could take another look at it all. I'm sure Molly wouldn't have wanted anything to get in the way of our big day. What do you say?'

I cannot dignify any of that with an answer and just stare at Mark in disbelief, wondering how he could be so cold as to talk about wedding planning after all that has happened. But then, as if reading my mind and realising that he should acknowledge the rather sizeable elephant in the room, he takes another step forward before speaking again. Only this time, there is no jovial lilt to his voice.

'Look, I get it. You're worried about what I said last night, about me possibly having something to do with Molly. If that's the case, then all I will say is that you should stop for a minute and have a serious think about what you do next.'

'What do you mean?' I ask him, one of my hands reaching out and gripping the doorframe beside me for extra support, as I suddenly feel seriously shaky.

'Well, if you do think I hurt Molly, then you might be thinking about telling somebody about that. The police, perhaps? The problem is that would be a very bad idea, and I'd advise against it. If you tell anybody that you think I killed Molly, then you would leave me with little choice.'

Mark glares at me, but I say nothing, inadvertently inviting him to go on.

'I don't want to hurt you, Kate. I want to marry you,' he says, his eyes looking me up and down as he speaks. 'So please be a good fiancée and do as I say; otherwise, well, you might be seeing Molly again much sooner than you thought.'

With that, Mark turns for the staircase, and as he goes down, he asks me if I would like some toast and a glass of orange juice.

But I don't respond.

I just retreat into the bathroom, lock the door and then stand by the sink, frozen in fear and wondering how I am going to get out of this relationship alive.

30

A lot can happen in ten days. A coroner can examine a body and record a verdict of accidental death, adding one more number to those statistics that say how many people have died falling down the stairs at home. A family, even through all the pain and grief, can make funeral arrangements for their lost loved one, ensuring a fit and proper send-off is given to the deceased in the appropriate fashion. And as well as all that, a frightened woman can return to work after taking a few days off, resuming her normal routine while ensuring she also sticks to the promise she was forced to make to her partner in which she must stay quiet and never tell anybody that he might have murdered somebody and got away with it.

Ten days.

Several devastated people.

One lost life.

But so far, it remains just one.

Not two.

Not me as well.

The sky is overcast, and there's rain in the air as I join the rest of the mourners at Molly's funeral. We make our way into the chapel, where the coffin resides, surrounded by flowers, a few symbols of religion and one framed photo showing the deceased at her best, smiling widely and looking beautiful with her children beside her, the picture of perfect happiness from a time when nobody could ever have imagined it would all end so soon.

I see Gary at the front of the chapel, having a quiet word with the woman who will be overseeing proceedings here today, while, only a short distance away from them, his children sit with their grandparents, some of them crying, some of them staring ahead in stony silence, but all of them united in their grief at what they have recently lost.

I offer a very weak smile to a couple of my friends when I see them, but any thoughts I had about going and sitting beside them are dashed when Mark takes a hold of my hand and leads me to a separate row of seats, ensuring I am sat with him and unable to talk easily to my closest confidantes at this difficult time.

When the service begins, I find it difficult to know where to look because there are simply too many upsetting sights that offer little comfort. As my eyes flit from the coffin to the photo to the family at the front and then to the memorial booklet in my hand that lists out the hymns for today as well as a brief bio of the life and times of Molly Ashgrove, I feel my vision clouding over with tears and require a tissue to restore its clarity again. But Mark is on hand to provide me with all the tissues I need, and even though I hate him and fear him in equal measure, I accept those tissues because this moment right here is not about me or him and the silent threats that hang between us. It is about Molly, my dear best friend, and the woman who is spoken about so eloquently and bravely by both her widow and her father before proceedings are wrapped up and the coffin is moved on into a private area where the family can say their last goodbyes in peace.

While Molly is laid to rest, the majority of mourners have been requested to move on to the venue for the wake, and we do just that, travelling to and then gathering in a large pub that offers refreshments as well as an opportunity for those in attendance to share their favourite memories of the deceased. While Mark might have successfully kept me away from my friends at the service, he stands little chance of doing it here, and after joining my friendship group at a table near the buffet stand, each of us tries to remember the good times while finding it impossible to acknowledge the bad time that we exist in right here and now.

Tales are told of Molly at university, at the workplace, on holiday abroad and at the weekends, and for several brief moments, a little light-hearted anecdote is what each of us needs to force a smile onto our faces and temporarily forget that there will be no more additions to our friend's life story. Mark stands beside me through it all, listening to each person speak and offering the appropriate response, be it laughter, respect or just keen interest. But he says nothing; I am always aware of his presence just near enough to me to keep tabs on anything that might come out of my mouth whenever I choose to speak.

But after a few glasses of wine, a small plate of food from the buffet and a very tiring time of focusing on such a heavy emotion as grief, there is a need for a change in conversation, and that's when my friend Tina brings up a subject that should lighten the mood a little.

And that subject is my wedding.

'So, just over a week to go until the big day,' she says with a smile, no doubt feeling a little sorry for me that my big day has ended up falling in the same time period as such a sad occasion as today.

'Yeah, it's come around quick. We're excited, aren't we?' Mark says, taking hold of my hand and encouraging me to reinforce what he has just said.

'Erm, yeah, can't wait,' I reply, but it's not very convincing, although everybody who hears me will automatically assume I'm just a little downbeat because my best friend won't be there to celebrate with me.

'We're going to give you the best day ever, like Molly would have wanted,' Tina says, and everyone else in the circle is in agreement, including Mark.

'Yeah, we'll be sure to acknowledge her absence, of course,' he says, still holding my hand but a little more tightly now. 'But we have to remember that it's supposed to be a celebration, and if Molly were there, she would have celebrated as much as anybody, so we should make sure to do the same in her honour.'

Mark then goes on to tell my friends how he has adapted his groom's speech to include Molly in it, a fact that elicits a positive reaction from them all, and they tell him that is very kind and that they are sure the speech will be great. But all of this is too much for me, which is why I make my excuses and head off to the toilets, the one place in this pub that Mark is unable to follow me and, therefore, the only place I might get a moment's respite from his awful presence.

Locking myself in one of the cubicles, I lean against the back of the door and take several deep breaths, doing everything within my power to try to calm down so I don't lose it here in front of so many people. While today should have been about nothing more than remembering my friend, I've spent most of it wondering if I should just suddenly blurt out that I think my fiancé killed her so that he is taken into police custody immediately to be questioned. But so far, I've chosen not to do such a dramatic thing, although it's less about not wanting to ruin the funeral and more about my fear that Mark might be able to make it through questioning without any charges being pressed and, therefore, ending up free to come out and punish me.

There is no evidence to tie him to Molly's death, despite my best efforts to try to find some. One of those efforts involved me going to the phone repair shop while I was on my lunch break at work yesterday and asking the tech specialists there to have a look and see if they could find any spy software installed on my phone. My hope was that if they could, I could potentially use that as evidence against Mark, telling the police that it was proof he is possessive of me and that he knew I was about to alert Molly to the fact he was abusing me. Then, armed with that information, the police would at least be aware that Mark was not just the happy, friendly guy who everyone else in this world seems to believe he is. But to my dismay, the tech expert who looked at my phone found no such software on my device, although he did say that didn't mean it hadn't been on there at some point previously. But that wasn't much help to me. Mark had obviously deleted it off my phone at some point since Molly's murder, thereby erasing something that could have made him less trustworthy in the eyes of the law. He must have done it during the very limited hours I've slept since my friend's death, and it's easy to regret not keeping a tight grip on my device whenever I closed my eyes.

Although it was a shame to learn that the spyware was gone, it did at least give me the confidence to use my phone again without fear of my partner snooping on everything I did with it, although so far, I haven't done much. If anything, I've been avoiding using it much because I don't want to see anything on it that will remind me of Molly. There are mainly photos of us, of course, but messages as well. But there was a moment a few days ago when I did go into the WhatsApp chat I had with Molly just to look at the last few messages I sent her and decide if there was enough within them to take to the police and show that I was afraid of Mark, and Molly had been tipped off about it, thereby giving him a motive to hurt her. But, to my shock, Mark had already deleted the last few messages I'd sent. There was also no easy way of anybody seeing the messages on Molly's phone because Gary told me her mobile had been broken in the fall, although I suspect it was actually Mark who made sure to smash it up before he left her body at the bottom of the stairs. Either way, he seemed to have covered all the angles, proving once again that he's one step ahead at every turn.

In need of a little distraction before leaving this cubicle and going back out there into the wake, I take my phone from my handbag with the intention of scrolling absent-mindedly through the Celebrity section of a newspaper's website, hoping for a little trashy gossip from the lives of the rich and famous to restore my mind to a more peaceful state. But no sooner have I looked at my phone than I see a missed call notification on the screen, from a number I do not recognise. It was only a minute ago that this person tried to ring me, but I missed it because I put my phone on silent mode, just like everybody else at the funeral, so as not to accidentally interrupt the proceedings.

I'm just debating whether to try to call this number back when my phone rings again, so I answer it and say hello, wondering who it could be.

'Kate? Hi, it's me,' the voice says from the other end of the line, but in case I'm still unsure as to their identity, the speaker gives me their name as well.

'Tristan.'

31

I t's the day after I watched my best friend being laid to rest, and after being excused from work to attend Molly's funeral, I have been back in the office to carry out my professional duties once again. But that's not the only thing I have to do today, and once the clock hits five and I'm walking out the door, I'm more than ready for the real reason I found the energy to get out of bed this morning.

I'm going to meet Tristan.

To say it was a shock to hear his voice over the phone yesterday would be an understatement, but no sooner had I gotten over that than he had explained what was going on. He told me he was calling me from a payphone because Tess made regular checks on his personal phone, and he didn't want her to find out he was reaching out to me. Then he apologised for how he'd left things with me before, which meant that he said sorry for basically telling me to leave him alone after we had seemed to make good progress during the lunchtime meet-up we had. And, finally, he told me that he couldn't forget about what we had discussed and that he wanted to see me again because things were only getting worse with his fiancée, and he wasn't sure whom else to turn to.

He then asked if we could meet, and despite knowing the risks it entailed, I said yes before I could change my mind. That is why I am now on my way to the meeting point, which is the Carter Arms, a pub I am becoming more than familiar with. But while it's close to the dress shop where our paths first crossed, it's far enough away from either of our workplaces that we're not risking being seen by anybody we know. Tristan is clearly afraid of Tess finding out that he is meeting me again, while I am more than a little anxious about what might happen if Mark was to discover that I'm seeing Tristan, but we should be on safe ground here.

I have already furnished my partner with a reasonable excuse as to why I will be home late tonight, telling him that I'm going to meet one of Molly's friends who wasn't able to make it to the funeral yesterday but wanted to do her own reminiscing with me because we knew each other well from various parties over the years. Of course, Mark wasted no time in giving me yet another warning, reminding me that things would be very bad for me if I were to breathe one word of what he might have done to anybody else. But I assured him I wouldn't, and he believed me, though why wouldn't he when he presumes that I value my life and don't want to risk losing it?

As I make my way to the meeting point with Tristan, I recall how afraid he sounded on the phone yesterday. He wouldn't tell me exactly how things had got worse with Tess, only that they had, and I could hear in his voice that he was a man who feared for his future, the fact he was cowering in a payphone booth as he spoke to me only reinforcing that.

But I expect him to tell me everything tonight, removing most of the questions I have and, essentially, only leaving me with one.

Will I tell him everything too?

I know the dangers to myself if I do because Mark has not been shy in telling me about them, but would Tristan also be in danger if I was to enlighten him about my fiancé possibly killing my best friend? I'd hate to drag him into this mess as well, but he's dragging me into his, not that I'm disappointed about that. The fact that he called me at what sounded like his lowest point tells me that I made an impression on him. He clearly trusts me, and I assume it's because he sees me as a kindred spirit, someone who knows what it is like to be trapped in a relationship that seems so perfect to the outside world. That means things take less explaining with me, or perhaps less justifying, and most importantly, he knows he will not be judged by me if he shares anything that some people might consider to be embarrassing.

He clearly trusts me, so maybe I can trust him too.

If so, perhaps there is a way out of this for the pair of us.

I make it to the pub just after 6 p.m., and when I go inside, I see that Tristan is already here, seated at a booth in the corner and forlornly staring at the top of his pint. But despite recognising him, I can't fail to notice that there are some changes in his appearance since the last time I saw him, which was almost a fortnight ago. He looks to have lost a little weight in that time, and his haggard complexion suggests a serious lack of sleep over the last two weeks. While a female passer-by would no doubt still call him attractive if questioned about such a thing, I know this hand-some man is a shell of who he was the first time I saw him, and who knows, even then, he might already have been suffering.

As I approach the booth, Tristan is in such a daze that he doesn't notice me until I am right in front of him, but when he sees I'm here, he smiles and thanks me for coming. I tell him it was no trouble at all before quickly ordering myself my own drink and then sitting down to hear what Tristan has to say, but before he can get into that, I can't help but comment on his quite disturbing appearance.

'You look awful,' I say, not expecting that to be a news-flash to him, and sure enough, it's not.

'Tess has got me on a strict diet and exercise regime for the wedding,' he replies, although the way he sounds makes it seem less like a health kick and more like starving him into exhaustion..

'That's not all,' Tristan says, looking around the pub to make sure no one is looking at us before he rolls up the sleeves on his shirt, revealing several bruises and cuts on his forearms.

'Oh my God! Tess did that to you?' I ask before he tells me to keep my voice down and covers up his injuries before anybody else can see them.

'She's got worse,' he admits before he shakily picks up his pint and takes a gulp. 'Maybe it's because the wedding is getting nearer, or maybe it's because of what happened with you, but she's more aggressive now. I could handle her slap-ping me and occasionally throwing something at me, but it's escalated. I woke up the other morning to her hitting me on my arms, and two nights ago, she came at me with a knife. I got all those cuts when I put my arms up to protect myself.'

I'm horrified at what I'm hearing, although the shock of

this is temporarily taking my mind off the awful situation in my own home life.

'The incident with the knife was what made me call you yesterday,' Tristan tells me, looking so weak and vulnerable that I just want to reach across this table and hug him. 'I just wish I'd done what we agreed after we last met. I'm so sorry for going back on my promise to you. I was just scared. I couldn't do it.'

'That's okay,' I say, reaching out for his hand and being careful not to brush against his forearm because it certainly looks very sore underneath that shirt of his. But he moves his hand away, and the nervous glance he takes around the pub straight after that movement makes me think he is just ultra-paranoid about anybody seeing us who might recognise him who might then go and tell Tess.

'I understand,' I say, not letting that stop me from trying to help him. 'I know how hard it is to get away from somebody, no matter how much you might want to.'

'What about you?' Tristan asks me then, looking at my glass of wine that I still haven't taken a single sip from because I've been far too busy listening to him.

'What about me?'

'Have you done it? Have you left your partner?'

I realise then that because Tristan told me to leave him alone, a wish I obeyed, he has no idea what might have gone on in my life since we were last together. He might presume that I kept my end of the bargain and left Mark, and because of that, I'm now free and clear of all the trouble at my end.

But that assumption could not be further from the truth.

I have no idea what the best way is to tell Tristan about all the crazy happenings recently, so I just blurt it all out as quickly as I can, although by the time I have finished, I am more than ready to take a first gulp of my drink.

Tristan looks just as horrified as I presume I did when he told me his story, but, based on what he says next, he seems to have forgotten all about his problems.

'You need to go to the police! If Mark killed Molly, then he has to pay for it!'

'I can't go to the police. I have no evidence, and then he'll kill me!'

'But you can't just let him get away with it!'

'You can't let Tess get away with what she is doing either! But you're scared, aren't you? Well, so am I!'

I didn't mean to shout at Tristan, but I just got a little frustrated that he seemed to think he had such a simple solution to my problem when, in fact, I am just as frightened as he is, if not more. As far as I can tell, so far, his partner has only hurt another person.

But my partner has actually killed another person.

'I'm sorry,' he says when I've calmed down. 'You're right. It's not easy to do what needs to be done. I know that better than anyone. I've been a coward for too long. But you're not being a coward here, you're genuinely in fear for your life, and I can't even imagine what that must feel like.'

I appreciate that Tristan is trying to give me a pass for not reporting my partner yet now that he knows the full story, but the way I see it, he deserves a pass just as much as I do.

'Aren't you in fear for your life too?' I ask him. 'Tess came at you with a knife and cut your arms. What's to stop her from stabbing you next time? Like you said, it's escalating, so who knows how far she will go?'

Tristan doesn't look like he wants to openly admit that I

am right, but he doesn't disagree either. All he can do is suggest another drink, and this time, our beverages are drunk much more quickly, the seriousness of our situation making us both thirsty.

But while alcohol very rarely offers the answers to tricky dilemmas in most normal realms of life, in this instance, the liquid courage it provides us gradually starts to lower our inhibitions. It does so to the point where we think we might see a way out of this, and by the time we're on our third drinks, we are forming a plan.

'What if we just walked into a police station together,' Tristan muses as he stares into his beer. 'Both just ask to speak to someone and then tell them. We'll say we need protection, and they'll surely give it to us, right?'

'I really want to do that,' I admit, meaning it. 'But what evidence do we have? I guess you could show them the bruises on your arms, but Tess could just deny it, couldn't she?'

I think I've just posed a good question to Tristan, but rather reluctantly, he reaches into his pocket and takes out his mobile phone. Then he shows me something on it. It's a video, and while it takes me a few seconds to figure out what I'm seeing, it gradually becomes obvious.

He has recorded footage of Tess hitting him.

'I could show them this,' he says. 'I took it last weekend when I knew she was in one of her bad moods and was likely to do something about it. She has no idea I have it. I guess I thought I could use it against her one day. Threaten her with it, and then she might stop. But that's a terrible idea. I should just show it to the police and leave it up to them to sort out.'

'That's brilliant!' I say, genuinely pleased that he has such evidence to trip up his partner. But my happiness is tinged with the realisation that I lack such a thing on Mark, a fact that Tristan obviously picks up.

'You could do the same thing to Mark,' he suggests. 'Secretly record him and get him to talk about Molly and what he did to her. Then he'll be screwed! That's all the evidence you'll need, right?'

I think about it, and while it does sound like a good plan, it also sounds incredibly dangerous, but again, it's as if Tristan reads my mind.

'I could come to the house with you and wait outside,' he says. 'If you're in any danger, then you could signal to me or something, and I could intervene.'

'No, you can't do that!' I say, surprised he would offer, but also deeply touched that he would be willing to potentially put himself in harm's way for me.

'Hey, we're a team, aren't we?' Tristan asks, smiling at me, and it's the first time he looks genuinely happy since I sat down here tonight. 'I let you down last time, but I want to make it up to you. So what do you say? How about we go and catch Mark confessing to his crime, and then we go to the police station and let them deal with our abusive partners once and for all?'

It might be the alcohol talking, but both of us are in on the scheme, and as we leave the booth and head for the door, I can't believe we're actually going to do this.

All I have to do is get Mark talking about Molly while secretly recording the conversation, and then I can run from the house, join Tristan outside, and we'll go straight to the police.

It's a solid plan, and it just might work.

At least that's what I thought until we left the pub and saw who was waiting for us outside.

32

'Hello, Kate,' Mark says before turning his attention to the man standing beside me. 'And who might you be? Tristan, perhaps?'

I cannot believe it. Why is Mark here? How did he find me?

And what is he going to do now?

All my intentions of going straight from this pub to home to secretly record Mark's confession evaporate as I stare at my fiancé and try to gauge what he will do next. Meanwhile, Tristan says nothing, but he must have figured out who this is based on how afraid I now am.

'I guess you're surprised to see me,' Mark says smugly, revelling in being one step ahead of me yet again.

But how has he done it? I know the spy software is no longer on my mobile phone. so how does he know that I spoke to Tristan yesterday and planned to come here to meet him?

Then I figure it out. It's actually quite simple.

'You followed me from my office?' I ask Mark, and he nods to let me know that I'm right.

'I didn't believe your story about going to meet one of Molly's friends,' he tells me, making me regret ever concocting the story in the first place. 'Especially when I'd already been having my suspicions that something had been going on with you and another man. So I left work early, went to your office and waited for you to leave. Then I followed you here, and I've been waiting for you to come back out of this pub ever since.'

I cannot believe that during the whole time I was inside with Tristan, trying to come up with a way to get rid of Mark once and for all, he was standing patiently on the other side of the door, waiting to make his grand appearance.

'We're not having an affair,' Tristan says, suddenly speaking.

'Oh, you're not? That's a relief,' Mark fires back quickly, looking amused that Tristan has dared to speak up. 'Although I wouldn't expect you to readily admit to it, would I? Of course, you're bound to deny anything is going on.'

'No, it's true,' I say, praying he'll believe me. 'We've just had a drink together, but nothing is going on. There's no affair.'

'Just one drink, was it? You were in there for quite a while.'

'Okay, we had a couple,' I admit. 'But we are not having an affair. I am not cheating on you.'

I don't expect Mark to take my word for it, and based on how unpredictable he has often been, I am worried about the multitude of possible things he might do next. But to my great surprise, he doesn't get angry or threaten violence or demand I come home with him while telling Tristan to get lost and never come near me again. Maybe that's what Tess would do, but Mark seems to be taking a different route here.

Instead of looking angry, he actually looks upset.

And then, even more surprisingly, he is apologetic.

'I'm sorry for following you,' he says to me. 'And I'm sorry for not trusting you. But can you see why I was afraid? I don't want to lose you, but first I find out you're messaging another man, and now I find out you've been lying to me and pretending to be meeting friends when really you're going for drinks with him.'

This is not at all how I thought Mark would react. Rather than being the furious, jealous and jilted lover, he is being a heartbroken, humble and honest man, which makes it so much harder for me to get defensive and be on my guard with him. But I have to remember just how dangerous he can be, so after presuming that this is still all an act on his part, I remind Mark of Molly and what he did to her.

'You hurt my best friend,' I say, not caring that Tristan is with us as I say it to Mark. 'And you've been threatening me ever since. And now you expect me to believe that you love me and would do anything for me?'

'Yeah, I heard exactly what you did to Molly,' Tristan says, speaking up again, though this time, I really wish he wouldn't because it only confirms to Mark that I have let slip about his dark secret after promising him that I wouldn't tell another soul. 'You're a murderer, but you're going to pay for what you did.'

With that said, Mark has no reason now not to try to silence me and, by association, Tristan. But he doesn't attempt to do that. Instead, he surprises me again.

'Oh, Kate, I didn't actually kill Molly,' he says, speaking

quietly and shaking his head as if he has been an idiot to allow me to think such a thing. 'I was just hinting at it to scare you. Do you really think I'm capable of murder, never mind getting away with it? I'm not a killer. I'm not even violent. Tell me, when have I ever raised a finger to you?'

Barring the incident when he threw my phone against the wall, I can't think of one, and now seeing Mark like this makes me think he might be telling the truth, which only adds to my confusion.

'You were just hinting at it?' I repeat back to him for clarification.

'Yes, I knew you were unhappy and probably wanting to leave me, so I had to do something. It was stupid, I know that now, but I thought that if I could scare you, then you might just stay with me.'

'That is stupid,' Tristan agrees, but Mark doesn't argue.

'I don't want to lose you, Kate,' Mark goes on, and I think there might be tears in his eyes. 'I love you, and I want to marry you. I'll do anything for you. Anything.'

This situation gets stranger by the second, and now I have no idea what to think. But, as crazy as it sounds, I actually believe Mark when he tells me he didn't kill Molly because he's right in that he has not been violent before; graduating from throwing a phone at a wall to killing a person by pushing them down the stairs is a big leap.

'Can you forgive me?' Mark asks, looking pathetic, but the fact he isn't trying to one-up Tristan in some display of macho strength makes me even more inclined to believe that this is a display of honesty.

'I don't know,' I say, totally confused now, although Tristan leans into me and whispers a warning in my ear.

'You can't trust him,' he says. 'He could be lying. I've seen Tess act like this before too.'

That reminder is all I need to snap out of it and realise that Tristan is right. I cannot trust Mark. I couldn't trust him before, and I can't trust him now.

'It's over,' I tell my fiancé, looking him in the eye. 'I don't know if you did hurt Molly or not, but that's for the police to decide. Either way, I know what I want. I'm leaving you. The wedding is off.'

I feel good for saying all of that, and I feel even better knowing I have the extra insurance of Tristan standing beside me to protect me from whatever might happen next. But then Mark's demeanour changes, and suddenly I'm not feeling quite so confident about things.

That only gets worse when I see what Mark pulls out from inside his coat.

It's a knife.

'Mark, what are you doing?' I say as I see the glint of the blade as it catches one of the lights from the pub behind me, and if only I weren't so afraid, then I would get my body moving and run inside to get help. But I can't move, and neither can Tristan, and all the pair of us can do is watch Mark as he points the deadly weapon towards us.

'Plan B,' Mark says coldly. 'I tried to pretend to be weak, but the truth is I'm not. I did hurt Molly, and now I'm going to hurt you. Both of you.'

With that, Mark lunges forward, jabbing the knife towards me, but Tristan pushes me out of the way before narrowly avoiding the blade and attempting to wrestle it from Mark's control.

I watch on in horror as the two men scuffle, the knife going in and out of vision as I keep losing track of it between the two bodies that desperately want to have sole ownership of the weapon. It's hard to tell who has the upper hand, but one thing is for sure. Somebody is going to get seriously hurt in a second, and because I'm terrified it will be Tristan, I have to do something to stop this.

That's why I turn back to the pub and am just about to run inside and beg somebody to help when I hear a loud, ghastly groan.

Turning around, I catch sight of the knife again though this time the blade is not glinting silver.

It's red.

I have no idea whose blood it is until I see Tristan step back, and when he does, Mark falls forward onto the pavement in front of him, clutching his stomach as he goes. Then, as he lies in the gutter, he looks up at me, but when he goes to speak, the only thing that comes out of his mouth is more blood.

I'm stunned to see that Mark is wounded, possibly mortally so, and as Tristan recoils in shock at what he has just done, I quickly look around the quiet street to find out if anybody else has seen what happened. But there's nobody out here, at least not yet anyway, but that will likely change any moment now.

'We need to call an ambulance!' I say as Mark gasps and grows quieter, his movements lessening as his breathing slows, because as much as I might have hated this man for the way he treated me, I have never wished him to come to harm like this.

'No!' Tristan says as he suddenly snaps out of the trance he has been in ever since he saw what he did to Mark.

'What do you mean? We need to get help! He's going to die!' I say as I fumble for my phone in my handbag. But

Tristan rushes to me and stops me from calling for the emergency services.

'Please, you can't call anybody. I can't go to prison for this!'

'You won't go to prison! He was attacking you. It was self-defence!'

'No, we can't risk it. What if the police don't believe me?'

Mark is lying still and silent now, and while blood continues to leak from his stomach onto the pavement, I sense that my fiancé is no longer with us. I guess I'm in total shock because I'm not crying or doing much of anything at the moment other than staring at the body on the ground and wondering if all of this is my fault. Mark might have brought this on himself by turning up here with a knife and threatening us, but he was only here because I came to meet Tristan. If I'd just gone home as planned, then he would still be alive now.

'Oh my God, he's dead,' Tristan says, putting his hands on his head. 'I've killed him!'

I can't disagree with that, and even though there are extenuating circumstances, the fact of the matter is that Mark is dead because Tristan stabbed him.

'We need to get out of here,' Tristan says, well aware of the trouble he is in now. 'I'll get rid of the knife. You go home and then phone the police later tonight saying that Mark hasn't come home from work, and you have no idea where he might be. Okay?'

'What? No!'

'You have to, Kate! It's either that or I go to prison for this! Please help me!'

'Tristan, no! Running away isn't the right thing to do!'

I want to go into the pub and tell somebody what has just

happened out here, but Tristan grabs my arm, and when I look into his eyes, I see such fear behind them that it scares me.

'Please, Kate. Just go home.'

'I can't. It's not right.'

But Tristan doesn't listen to me because the sound of a car in the distance spooks him, and he suddenly sets off running.

I'm alone with Mark's body then and have no idea what to do. And that's when I notice something lying on the road several yards away from where Mark fell. When I go to see what it is, I find that it is Tristan's phone. He must have lost it in the scuffle.

I call after him to tell him what he's left behind, but he's already gone, and as I hear the unseen car getting nearer, I have to make a quick choice.

Do I stay here and try to explain this to the police?

Or do I copy Tristan and just make a run for it?

Before I have fully had the chance to appreciate the seriousness of what I am doing, my legs are moving beneath me, and just like the man who killed Mark, I am fleeing the scene.

33

I was planning on running all the way to the nearest tube station, but no sooner have I made it on to a main road than I'm struck by the thought of all the CCTV cameras in the area, so I decide to try to draw less attention to myself and walk instead. It's not easy slowing down because now that I've fully committed to leaving the crime scene behind, I feel like I should be getting away from it as quickly as possible. But I resist the urge to sprint again and, instead, choose to mix in with all the other people walking towards the entrance to the train station, ensuring I look just like one of them, a commuter or tourist on their way home after a busy day in the city.

But of course, I am nothing like them. We could not be more different.

That's because they are going home after finishing work or taking a few photographs of a famous landmark.

Meanwhile, I'm going home after witnessing my fiancé get stabbed and be left to die on a quiet street outside a busy pub.

The paranoia I feel about somebody in that pub potentially having seen what happened is almost too much to bear as I squeeze myself onto one of the escalators. But the fact the pub has stained-glass windows, which allow light in but are not see-through, gives me hope nobody inside saw what happened outside.

But my paranoia only worsens as I descend deeper into the station, going underground, beneath the streets of London where up above my head right now, so much is going on. Delivery vans race to drop off their next parcel. Taxi drivers rush to their next customer's address. And police cars and ambulances zigzag all over the city limits, reaching crime scenes, tending to victims and then, ultimately, opening investigations into what might have happened before they got there.

I feel like I could be sick as I reach the platform and wait for the next train to arrive, a train that I urgently need to get away on because only once I'm on it will I really feel like I'm getting out of here. I wonder how far Tristan has got in making his own journey home tonight, no doubt just as stressed as I am and just as eager to walk through his front door and then act like nothing happened.

But as I hear a loud rumble farther down the tunnel that tells me my train is barrelling towards me, I know that I only have a few more hours of being able to act like nothing happened. That's because at some point, I'm going to have to call the police and tell them that Mark has not come home, expressing fake concern and worry about where he might be. Then I'll have to keep up my act as they look for him before, ultimately, they'll come to my house and give me the bad news, followed up by a simple question.

Mark is dead.

Do I have any idea who might have hurt him?

I couldn't care less about finding a seat on the train and care more about just being on it when it starts to move again, and as I hold the handrail and watch the doors close, I feel like I can finally breathe. I'm leaving London or at least the part of the city where Mark's body is located.

Will the distance between me and him make me appear more innocent?

I hope so.

Otherwise, I'm going to be spending a long time behind bars.

As the train carries me home, I think about the chain of events that led to Tristan stabbing Mark in self-defence and wonder how easily things could have been so different. Mark could have stabbed Tristan. He could have stabbed me. We're the innocent ones in all this, yet we could have easily been the ones who died. With that in mind, it's a relief that things turned out the way they did, though it's only a temporary relief because at the end of the day, the police won't give a damn about anything other than finding out why somebody lost their life today.

I try not to make much eye contact with anybody else on the train as it gets closer to home. Whenever I do, I feel as though they are looking at me because they know my secret. It's obvious that paranoia will be my only companion tonight, and as I leave the train and start making the short walk back to my house, I wonder how Tristan is going to handle his paranoid thoughts this evening. But I can't ask him because not only did he tell me not to contact him just before he ran away but because I also have his phone in my possession, the one he dropped as he was wrestling for the knife with Mark.

I wonder if he's noticed it missing yet. If he has, then I bet he thinks it is lying by the body and will lead the police right to his doorstep. He may even have gone back to try to find it on the pavement. But I've got it, ensuring the police can't link him to the crime scene, at least not yet anyway. I'm not sure what I'll do with the extra phone that now sits in my handbag beside my own as I unlock my front door, go inside and quickly slide the latch across to make myself feel safe.

If the police do come to arrest me soon, then I doubt the latch will slow them down too much, but just having it in place makes me feel a little better. All I want to do now is get into bed, fall asleep and wake up to find out that this whole night was just a bad dream. But instead, I do something a little more productive. I change out of my clothes, take a hot shower, pour myself a strong drink and then turn on the TV to see if there are any news reports about a man's body being found on the streets of London.

There's nothing yet, but that's surely only because the media haven't got hold of the story. There's no way the police haven't already been alerted to the body; it's right outside a busy pub where people are always coming and going. Somebody will have seen it and called 999, and a murder investigation will no doubt already be underway.

But are there any suspects yet?

As the sky gets darker outside and the time on the clock gets later, I wonder if Tristan is glued to the news like I am, waiting for the first mention of the terrible event he was a part of this evening. I also think about the advice he gave me just before he left when he told me that I was to call the police when it got late to report my partner as having not come home from work.

I've already sent a couple of text messages to Mark's phone over the last few hours, asking him how his day was before sending him a follow-up message to enquire as to what time he might be back this evening and if everything is okay.

I wonder what the best time to make my phone call to the police will be, but as the clock nears midnight, I decide I've left it long enough, and with a trembling hand, I pick up my phone and call the police.

'Hi. I'm ringing because my partner hasn't come home from work yet, and he isn't replying to any of my messages. I'm worried about him.'

The operator at the other end of the line tells me not to worry and that she is sure that he is fine, which is such a ridiculous thing to say given what I already know, before she informs me that I am to call back tomorrow if there has been no change. Apparently, it's too early for Mark to be listed as missing, so even though I provide his name and physical description, there's very little they will do with it yet unless something serious comes to their attention.

I have a feeling it will.

After ending my call, I try not to think about the seriousness of what I have just done and, instead, tell myself that I am no longer in any danger. Mark was a bad person, and he was only getting worse, so the world is a better place without him in it. However, just thinking that doesn't make it easier for me to go to bed and try to get some sleep, so I sit up all night on the sofa, watching the 24/7 news channels and waiting for any word on my fiancé's body.

It's just after 6 a.m. when I receive that word.

As the sun rises outside my window and the majority of people in the country start waking up to begin yet another day, my world is spinning out of control as I sit and listen to the newsreader tell whoever might be watching that a man's body was found outside the Carter Arms pub at 19:24 yesterday. The deceased is believed to have died as the result of a stab wound to his abdomen, but the police are not releasing the identity until the man's loved ones have been informed. As well as that, the police have not yet recovered the murder weapon and are appealing for anybody who might have been in the area at the time to come forward.

That's the moment I turn off the television because not only have I seen and heard enough, but I need to start getting ready.

I need to get ready for when the police come to my house to tell me that my fiancé is dead.

34

I should be on my way to work by now. I should be on the train with all the other commuters. And I should soon be listening to my colleagues tell me how there's not long to go now until my wedding day and how I must be incredibly excited.

But none of those things are happening. That's because I'm still sitting in my quiet house, and having just messaged my manager to tell her that I won't be in today due to Mark not coming home last night, I am not expected at my desk anytime soon. But I'm also here because I know I'm going to be receiving visitors at any minute, and as I wait nervously for them, I pace around my living room and try to visualise the conversation I'm about to have so that I might be somewhat prepared for it when it occurs.

First of all, I'm going to be given the bad news that Mark is dead.

What's the best way for me to act when I hear that? I should be devastated, of course, because any fiancée would be if they heard their partner was gone. That means I'll have to act shocked, then start crying, but I'll have to do a good job because this is no time for primary school acting skills. The police have to believe that I did not know about Mark being dead already, just as much as they need to believe that I am some normal, unassuming woman who has had her world turned upside down and whom they feel incredibly sorry for because I surely don't deserve any of it.

Okay, so let's say I can get through that first part. Once the tears have stopped for a moment and I've 'calmed down', I will probably be expected to ask them what happened.

How did Mark die?

He was stabbed? Oh my God, who would do such a thing?

Do I know why he was outside that pub? No, I've got no idea. Do you?

The police will surely be closely monitoring me and studying everything I say and do to try to ascertain whether I am telling them the truth, but I will be studying them just as closely because I want to find out every single thing that they know.

Will Tristan's name come up? What if it does? Should I pretend not to know him or confess to everything then?

I'm doing my best to envision my upcoming conversation with the police going well for me, ending in me watching them leave my house with my freedom intact. I know there are many sports people who espouse the virtues of visualising, believing it can improve their performance in the big game if they have already run through all the possible outcomes in their head beforehand.

But the question is, will positive visualisation work in this scenario?

The knock at the door tells me I'm just about to find out.

There are two police officers here to see me, and after

they have asked to come in, they get to the reason for their visit, informing me of Mark's body being discovered with sorrowful expressions and uncomfortable postures.

Just like I imagined doing it, I recoil in horror, put my hands over my wide-open mouth and then start crying, praying that I look every bit the heartbroken wife-to-be who has just had all her future hopes and dreams come crashing down around her.

I guess the police officers buy it because they offer me tissues and explain that extra support will be provided to me during this difficult time. I wish they would just leave it there, but then the younger of the two officers asks me a question. He's clearly ambitious or just simply overeager to get something he might be able to pass on to his superior in the hopes of getting a promotion one day, but whatever it is, he wants to know if Mark had any enemies.

I react as if such a suggestion is ridiculous and say no, but the officer doesn't stop there.

'Do you know why Mark was in that part of London last night?' he asks then. 'Because, from what we know, that area is quite far from his workplace, so something must have made him deviate from his normal routine.'

Yes, something did make him deviate from his normal routine, alright. He thought I was cheating on him, and after he followed me to that pub, he tried to attack me and the man I was with with a knife. But the knife got turned on him, and now he's dead, the pair of us hope to get away with what we did.

Is that okay?

Does that answer your question, officer?

But of course, I don't say any of that as I shake my head and say I have no idea what Mark was doing there last night.

The older officer, clearly aware that it's far too early in

my grieving process to be answering any more questions, politely ends the exchange there, standing up to leave and taking the younger officer with him. But before they can go, I have one question for them.

'Did anybody see what happened?' I ask before stifling a few sobs with my wet tissue.

The officers share a glance before looking back at me as they shake their heads.

'No. No witnesses have come forward yet.'

I want them to leave now so I can let out a deep breath and maybe even fist-pump the air to celebrate this little piece of good news, but just then, the older officer speaks again.

'But it's still early days yet. We've made an appeal, so if anybody did see what happened, I'm sure they will come forward. And I'm confident somebody will. After all, there are a lot of vantage points around there, so somebody must have seen something.'

They leave on that note, and after watching them go, I close the front door and think about all those vantage points. All the windows that overlooked that section of the street. The alleyways and corners around which anybody could have been lurking. And of course, the damn pub that was certainly busy when I left it and only a few yards away from where Mark was stabbed.

But did anybody see?

Or am I okay?

I guess only time will tell.

Well aware that the next few hours and days are going to move by at a snail's pace as I wait to see if any witnesses do come forward, I figure I am best to keep myself as busy as possible. One way of doing that is to do what any normal person would do after being told that their partner has just been killed, and that is to inform my family and nearest friends so they can rally around me and offer support.

While I do that and receive plenty of visitors, I also receive a visit from the grief counsellor I was promised by the police, and that keeps me occupied for a couple of hours as she asks me how I am coping before running through a couple of techniques that are designed to help me survive this awful time. I'm not sure how good the techniques would be if I were genuinely devastated about Mark's loss, but as someone who was actually glad to see the back of him, albeit in dramatic circumstances, I tell the counsellor that her advice is much appreciated and is already making a difference for me.

There is also the not-so-small matter of Mark's funeral to arrange, but, thankfully, much of the organisation of that is handled by Mark's family, who are united in their grief but also united in how oblivious they all are as to the nasty piece of work their loved one actually was.

And last but not least, there is one more thing that needs taking care of. My wedding, or, rather, *the cancellation of my wedding.*

What's more tragic than a woman losing her partner? A woman losing her partner just before their wedding, of course. That's why everybody has rallied around me to help deal with the cancellation of everything from the venue to the catering to the DJ, making sure I receive no phone calls or deliveries connected to what was supposed to be my big day in order to preserve my already fragile state of mind.

As for the dress, having already committed to its purchase, I had presumed I'd be stuck paying it off for the foreseeable future. So imagine my surprise when my mum told me that she had spoken to the dress shop about returning it for a possible refund and been told that given the unusual and awful circumstances, the order could be deleted, and I wouldn't owe them another penny. Chrissy obviously took pity on me and cancelled the order, because I never got the chance to actually walk down the aisle in my dress, and I must take the time to thank her for that when things have settled down. At some point, I'll have to return the dress that is currently hanging up on a special stand in my bedroom. The shop has said they will arrange for it to be collected, and I will need to get around to organising that because I imagine Chrissy's patience will only last so long if I don't. But for now, I've got bigger things to think about, and that's because the police are still looking into Mark's apparent murder.

The thing is, as the days go by, I start to hear less and less from them. They have no witnesses, nor do they have any suspects, and after I have somehow managed to get through Mark's funeral without any problems and the attention from family and friends slowly starts to die down, I think Tristan and I might just get away with this.

It's at that point that I start spending less time thinking about my late partner and more time thinking about the man who might be my next one.

My wedding might be off now, but what of Tristan's?

Is his big day still going ahead?

If it is, am I too late to stop it?

35

I 've been wanting to contact Tristan and not only find out if the police have spoken to him but ask him what is happening between him and Tess. More specifically, I want to know if he still plans to marry her or if he is going to stick to the original plan he had before Mark interrupted us, and leave her after so much physical abuse. But because he dropped his phone and I have it now, I no longer have a number to contact him on. That means I can't call or message him, and even assuming he has bought a new phone by now, it won't have my number saved in it, so he can't message me either. There's always Instagram, I suppose, but I doubt he'd risk contacting me on there. Not with Tess and her means of keeping tabs on him.

Therefore, the only way I have of speaking to him is to go to his house, but that seems like too big a risk. Not only is it unlikely that I could speak to him without Tess around, but there is still a police investigation underway, and the two of us should not be linked until that's over if we can help it. But despite all that, it's impossible to forget about Tristan. It's not only the fact that we made a pact to leave our abusive partners at the same time that makes me want to see him again. It's also because during the times we spoke, I felt a real connection with him, and I'm sure he felt it too. Because of that, I have this feeling that won't leave me alone.

It's the feeling that the two of us could be together.

But that can't happen if he goes ahead with his wedding.

It's the day before Tristan is scheduled to marry, and yet another day when the police have not come to arrest either of us, when I have an idea. It's an idea that takes me back to the mobile phone shop to see my old friend Ricky again. This time, the task I have for him is a slightly tricky one because it's not my phone that I am asking him to look at.

It's somebody else's.

I want him to look at Tristan's phone.

Or, more specifically, I want him to unlock it so I can access it and see if there's anything on there that might tell me if the wedding is still going ahead.

I had a go at cracking the four-digit code a few days ago, but that didn't work, and now the battery has died, so I can't even try anymore. It's a different make from my phone, so I don't have the right charger for it, but I'm hoping Ricky can help me with that and much more as I smile at him as I enter the shop.

'Wow, back again? Either you're really unlucky with phones, or I'm beginning to think you might have a crush on me.'

I roll my eyes at Ricky's joke before I tell him my problem.

'I've got this phone that I haven't used in a while,' I say, showing him Tristan's mobile, which I want him to think belongs solely to me. 'The problem is, I've lost the charger for it. Also, I've forgotten the PIN for it. Is there any way you can help me?'

Ricky takes the phone from me and has a look at it before telling me that finding a charger is not a problem. In fact, he has one in his drawer right here, and seconds later, the phone is filling up with power. But the bigger problem is accessing the phone if I don't have the code.

'How can you forget the code?' he asks me. 'Isn't it the same one as your current mobile?'

'No, unfortunately not,' I tell him, trying to look as sad about that as I can manage. 'I was trying to be clever and more security-conscious by using different codes, but I've gone and forgotten what it is now. Is there anything you can do?'

'Not really.'

This isn't going the way I want it to, and I'm just about to try a little flirting to see if that will get me anywhere when Ricky has a quick check over his shoulder before leaning into me.

'That's the official answer anyway. But there is something I can do. For £100 I'll unlock it.'

'One hundred pounds?'

That seems a bit steep to me, but then Ricky explains why.

'Technically, we're not supposed to do this for customers.'

'Why is that?'

'Because if someone doesn't know the PIN to a phone, then usually it means it's not their phone.'

I get it. Ricky is sceptical of my story and doubts the phone I want him to help me unlock is mine, so rather than dwell on that any longer, I quickly accept the price and allow him to get on with his work.

While I wait for him to do his work on Tristan's phone, I notice that I have a missed call on my own phone, and for a moment, I am terrified that it is the police trying to get a hold of me to tell me that they'd like me to come in for questioning. But I breathe a sigh of relief when it turns out that it's just Miranda checking in on me to see how I am doing since the funeral. As she offers me her sympathy again as well as condolences on behalf of everybody we work with, I feel a pang of guilt that so many people are worrying about me while I'm here spending my time worrying about Tristan and what might be happening with him. But I ensure my secret stays safe and chat to Miranda for twenty minutes or so until she tells me she has to get back to work, and after I've ended the call, I see that Ricky is ready for me again.

'All done,' he says as he hands me the phone. 'Just enter 1234 and you'll be in. I advise you change that as soon as possible though.'

'Of course,' I reply before trying the code and being relieved when it works.

After settling my bill and thanking Ricky, who gives me a sly wink as I leave the store, because he surely knows by now that the phone he just unlocked does not belong to me, I go outside before taking a proper look at the device I can now access.

The first thing I do is check the messages, and when I do, I see several from people who I presume are Tristan's friends, and all of them are saying the same thing.

Can't wait for your big day, man!

Not long now! I hope you're ready to down some shots!

How's the speech going? Please tell me you haven't left it to the last minute like I did!

By the sounds of things, Tristan's wedding is still very much on, which is more than a little disappointing. I get further confirmation of that when I check his emails and see that there is a reminder message in there from a suit shop telling Tristan the time that he and his groomsmen are to come and collect their wedding attire ahead of the big day. Yep, it's definitely not been cancelled yet.

It's impossible for me not to feel a sense of panic as I realise that Tristan is just days away from going through with his marriage to Tess despite what she has done to him and despite what he wanted to do before Mark confronted us with that knife. I don't want Tristan to suffer any more, not only because he doesn't deserve it or because he potentially saved my life by fighting Mark before he could do any harm to us with the knife.

It's because I want to be with him.

That's why I have to stop this wedding.

But how do I do that?

36

From where I'm sitting in Mark's car, I can just about see the entrance to the glamorous venue where Tristan and Tess are due to tie the knot within the next thirty minutes.

I've parked a safe distance away from the grand country house upon which over a hundred family and friends of the 'happy' couple are descending, and as I keep watch, I see many of the invited guests making their way inside. Men and young boys in smart suits and women and young girls in pretty dresses get out of taxis and enter the venue, all of them smiling and happy and no doubt looking ahead excitedly to a day of celebrating the upcoming matrimony that they are about to bear witness to. Behind them come the groomsmen, five men in perfectly fitted suits emerging from a sleek black car before the man I am here to see steps out onto the sprawling gravel driveway to join them.

Tristan looks every bit the handsome groom as he fastens the buttons on his blue waistcoat before posing for a picture with his five best friends, the wedding photographer kneeling in front of them all to capture the perfect shot that will end up in a photo album one day for people to look back at and remark on. At least that's the plan, but as I watch Tristan go inside to get ready to take his place at the end of the aisle, I know I am here to do everything in my power to prevent this wedding from reaching its expected conclusion.

I want to drive closer to the house now, up the driveway and past the luscious lawns and tall trees that surround it so I can get as close as possible to the venue. But I know I am best off waiting until everybody is inside before I make my approach, and that means I should stay where I am until the last few people are inside.

By my estimations, there are only a few more people to arrive.

The bridesmaids.

The father of the bride.

And the bride herself.

I wonder how Tess is feeling on the backseat of whichever car is bringing her to the venue now in time for her to make her grand entrance. Nervous? Excited? Or just eager to get this whole thing over with so she can trap Tristan in a lifetime of misery where she will be free to subject him to whatever abuse she wishes until death do them part. But the problem is, while most marriages should only end when one half of the couple sadly loses their life, those vows don't take into account the possibility of the wife being violent towards the husband, and because of that fact, I have to be the one to stop this whole charade before it can go any further.

I'd be lying if I said I wasn't disappointed in Tristan for not putting a stop to this himself, but he can't be blamed too much. He's terrified of Tess, similar to how I was with Mark, plus there's the fact that he might be thinking he's better off with her than me, because at least with her people don't end up dead and the police don't go around hunting for a murder suspect. But he's not better off with her, not by a long shot, and I just need to make him see that. But before he sees me, I need to stop this wedding, and it's almost time to do that because the star of the show is finally here.

I watch as a large pink car passes me by, and I catch a glimpse of several women on the backseat. But it's the pink car following just behind it that I'm more interested in because that is the one with Tess in it, and once the vehicles are parked at the front of the house, I see their occupants emerge.

There are four bridesmaids in total, and they pose for their obligatory photo before hurrying to go and take their positions inside, the ones in which they will make the first walk down the aisle before they are followed by the blushing bride herself and her father.

They are the two people I am watching now as they leave their vehicle, and when I get my first glimpse of Tess, I am caught in conflicting emotions.

I hate the woman with every part of my body, but, on the other hand, I can't help but acknowledge how beautiful she looks in her dress as she poses for her own photo in front of the pink car. The dress looks amazing on her, and I'm sure everybody waiting for her inside will think exactly the same thing when they see her.

Then she goes inside, her arm interlinked with her father's, a man who looks lovely himself in his own attire and a man who has surely dreamt of this day ever since he helped bring a little girl into the world. He doesn't deserve what is about to happen next. But I can't let that put me off, and that's why, now everybody is inside, I start the engine and drive forward, getting as close as I can to the country house and parking around the back of it, out of sight of the drivers of the pink cars at the front, before scurrying inside, making sure to use a different entrance than the one I saw everybody else walk through.

Having already had a look at the venue's website online, I know that the room in which the ceremonies take place has a large balcony that runs all around the top of it, and that's where I intend to view the proceedings from. I figure that will be the best place for me to stay out of view of all the guests down below but which will keep me close enough to the action so I can monitor what is going on and, most of all, make sure that my plan is actually working.

Finding a staircase, I go up it in the hope that it will lead me to the balcony, and after very quietly and slowly opening one of the several doors I see up on this first-floor landing, I find that's exactly where I am.

Tentatively stepping onto the balcony, I ever so carefully peer down just far enough to see what is below me, and when I do, I see the tops of the heads of over a hundred people, nearly all of them sitting in their seats and waiting for the ceremony to begin. The only people standing are those at the front of the room, at the 'altar' as such, even though this isn't a church. I spot Tristan easily amongst the people situated there, looking nervous as he stands beside his best man and waits for Tess to arrive. In front of him is the man who looks like he will be leading proceedings here today, and he leans over and whispers something to the anxious groom, no doubt offering a final few words of encouragement before everything gets underway.

The sound of the double doors opening at the back of the room suggests that time has now arrived.

As a soft ballad begins to play, and everybody turns around and cranes their necks to look at who is entering the room, I take one more step forward on the balcony before deciding that I've gone close enough to the edge and should go no farther if I want to avoid detection from below.

Joining everybody in looking towards the back of the room, I see the bridesmaids filing in, the four beautiful ladies in matching dresses smiling proudly as they pass the guests before they take their places at the front, on the opposite side of the aisle to where Tristan and his groomsmen wait. Then there is a brief pause in the music before another song starts to play, and it's at that moment that everybody in the room is instructed to stand, an order they all obey because they know exactly why they are being asked to do it.

The bride is ready to make her entrance.

I nibble nervously on my lip as I wait to see Tess enter the room, and when she does, there is a collective gasp of admiration around the room as everybody takes in the sight of the beautiful bride moving towards them in her flowing dress.

Tess smiles at all those in attendance as she passes them by while her father beams proudly beside her, and several people who watch them can't help but dab at their eyes with a tissue, such is the emotion they are feeling at this special time. Tristan shifts his feet a little awkwardly as Tess nears him before forcing a smile onto his face, one that must look genuine to everyone in attendance except me because I'm the only person who knows that he is wearing several cuts and bruises on his skin beneath that suit of his, and every single one of them was inflicted by the woman he is waiting for now.

As Tess reaches Tristan and takes her place beside him,

the music stops, and everybody in the room is now asked to be seated. But as I watch each of them do that, all their heads facing to the front of the room, ready to savour what happens next, I notice one little girl in a pink dress looking up at the balcony.

I've been seen.

What if she tells somebody?

What should I do?

Thinking fast, I put a finger to my lips in the hope that the little girl will get the message and not say anything to anybody about the lone woman up on the balcony watching from above. To my relief, the little girl seems to understand my request for privacy because she just smiles at me before looking towards the bride and groom, and with that, my presence here remains a mystery.

For a little while longer, anyway.

But as the ceremony begins and everybody in attendance is told exactly what this event means in the lives of both Tristan and Tess, I get ready to act because any minute now, the vows are due to start. However, before that, as is tradition, a question must be asked of all those in attendance.

'Is there anybody here who knows of any reason why these two people should not be wedded here today? If so, speak now or forever hold your peace.'

That's my cue.

That's the moment I take out Tristan's mobile.

And all I need to do then is press send.

37

I back away from the edge of the balcony and press my back to the wall as I hear a few phones beeping down below from those who forgot to switch their devices onto silent mode before the wedding began.

I stay there for a moment until I start to hear a bit of a commotion from down below, and as soon as more and more people see that they have a message, I expect the commotion to grow much larger.

And it does.

While there were collective gasps of awe when Tess made her appearance a moment ago, there are now collective gasps of shock as everybody starts watching the video on their phones, the video I just sent them from Tristan's mobile.

As the noise grows down below, I remain in hiding on the balcony, wondering what is going to happen next and whether or not the plan I've just put into action has worked.

But how can it not have done?

How can the wedding still go ahead now that everybody knows exactly what Tess does to Tristan behind closed doors?

It took a little while for the idea to come to me, but when it did, I knew it was a good one. Once I had access to Tristan's phone, I spent a long time going through it, looking at as much as I could to see if there was anything on there that could help me stop the wedding.

It was while I was looking in the video folder that I remembered what Tristan had told me.

He had secretly recorded Tess physically abusing him.

It didn't take me long to find that video, and once I watched it again, I knew it was the perfect thing to bring Tess down. The only thing I needed to do then was find the perfect way of using it against her. I initially considered just taking it to the police, but that felt like a very bad idea for several reasons. One, I'd have to explain how I came into possession of it, and therefore, a connection between myself and Tristan would be established, one that might not be so helpful if the police were ever able to find out we were both at the pub outside which Mark was found dead. And two, I was already on the police's radar with them having to keep me updated about Mark's death and subsequent investigation, so I didn't think it wise to give them another reason to pay me any attention.

The more I thought about it, the more I realised the perfect way to get back at Tess would be to show her up in front of all her family and friends and allow them to see exactly the kind of woman she is.

But how to do that?

How could I send the video to everybody at the wedding without their contact details?

Eventually, I realised what was staring me right in the

face or, should I say, what power I held in my hand now that I was in possession of Tristan's phone. The phone numbers for numerous people who would be at the wedding were stored on his device, and that was what gave me the ability to achieve what I wanted.

I could bring down Tess right in the middle of the ceremony, thus ensuring the wedding was ruined and stopped before it could go any further.

As the noise grows louder below, I hear a few people start to direct questions towards Tess, asking her if what they are seeing is real and how she could do such a thing. Braving a quick peek over the edge of the balcony again, I look down to see several people on their feet and pointing at Tess, while she seems to still have no idea what is going on and is asking to look at somebody's phone so she can see what is causing all the fuss. Meanwhile, Tristan looks just as confused, although when his best man taps him on the shoulder and shows him his phone, it slowly starts to dawn on the groom what is going on here.

While he will recognise the video, he won't know how it ended up being sent to everybody here, but it's too late to worry about that now because it's out there, and everybody in the room has seen it. Everybody except Tess, although that changes when I see her grab the phone out of a wedding guest's hand and look at it, and when she does, all the colour drains from her face, leaving her so pale that not even a professional make-up artist with years of wedding experience could return her cheeks to their natural colour.

I wonder what she is going to do now that she realises her secret is out. Will she run for the door? Stay and apologise? Try to explain herself and tell people that it's not what it looks like?

But she doesn't do any of those things.

All she does is turn to Tristan before lunging for him and attempting to hit him again.

Fortunately, Tristan's best man is on hand to pull his friend out of the way before Tess can land any more telling blows, and as the angry and aggressive bride is forcibly restrained by a man who looks like Tristan's father, it's obvious that everyone in the room knows who needs protecting here.

Tess is the bad guy, and she is treated as such, her arms held behind her back as everybody starts to leave the room, and Tristan heads somewhere safer while his furious bride continues to shout obscenities in his direction.

I decide that I should probably be on the move myself in case anybody comes up to this balcony, so I exit through one of the doors and find an empty room to hide in. But it's a room that offers me a view of the front of the venue, and as I watch the stunned guests spilling out onto the driveway below, I see that several of them are on their phones, making calls.

At first, I assume they are phoning for taxis to come and pick them up and take them home because it's clear that the celebrations are over for the day. But it's ten minutes later when I see the first police car arrive, and I realise then that a few of these people called 999 instead.

The arrival of a second police car corresponds with Tristan stepping out of the entrance below me, looking dazed and confused, although several guests are quickly on hand to offer their support to him. But there is still no sign of Tess as the police officers get out of their vehicles and begin to be enlightened about what is going on here by numerous

guests, who are eager to see the guilty party face conse-
quences for her actions.

I watch as one police officer looks at somebody else's
phone; presumably he's being shown the video that
everyone else has already seen. I guess I'm right about that
because no sooner has he looked at the phone than he goes
to speak to Tristan while instructing the other officers at the
scene to go inside the house, possibly to find Tess.

I hear her shouting downstairs a moment later, telling
somebody to get away from her, and I think how that surely
can't be a sensible way of dealing with any police officer who
wishes to speak to her. From the way she has behaved ever
since the video was made public, it seems she has lost all
control of herself. Rather than try to tactically stay calm and
pretend like the video is not what it looks like, she is acting
impulsively and only reinforcing the awful behaviour she
has demonstrated in the recording.

I get confirmation of just how badly Tess has acted a
moment later when I see her being led out of the house in
handcuffs, a police officer marching her towards one of the
cars, past all the guests, who stand and stare in a collective
stunned silence.

The bride is bundled into the back of the nearest police
car before the door is slammed shut, and she is driven away,
but just before she goes, I see her look up at the window I'm
standing at, and for a split second, the two of us make eye
contact. But then she is gone, and while I'm sure this won't
be the last I hear of Tess, for now, she is out of the picture.

That leaves me clear to talk to Tristan.

The only problem is there are so many other people
around, so I'm not sure how I'm going to get a quiet moment
with him. But I didn't come here today just to see Tess

destroyed. I also came to let Tristan know how strongly I feel about him, and I'm not going to leave until I've done that.

Spotting Tristan being led back inside the house by a friend who is no doubt keen to get him away from the glare of so many people who are still standing around and gawking at him, I sense my opportunity and quickly leave the room from which I just watched Tess being taken into police custody.

I hurry to the staircase that I ascended just before the wedding started, and when I look down, I see Tristan being shown into a room. At that point, the friend asks him if he would like a glass of water, and Tristan says yes, and as the friend goes to get it, he closes the door to the room that Tristan is in, giving the poor groom a moment's peace.

Rushing down the staircase because I don't have much time to waste, I reach the door to the room and take a deep breath. Then I enter, boldly and confidently, not allowing any doubt to creep in now because I've already come this far, and there's no sense in leaving without at least trying out the final part of my plan.

Tristan looks up when he sees the door open again, no doubt expecting to see his friend reappearing with that glass of water. But it's not him he sees.

It's me.

'Kate?' he utters, completely stunned at my appearance. 'What the hell are you doing here?'

I don't say anything because I know it shouldn't take long for the metaphorical penny to drop, and sure enough, I'm right.

'It was you who sent the video to everybody,' Tristan says, piecing it together, and I nod to confirm that he is correct, but while I'm sure he has a million other things to say to me, I'm the one who needs to get something out first.

'I know this is crazy, and I know we should probably stay away from each other for a while until everything settles down again, but I just wanted you to know that whatever happens, I want to thank you for what you did with Mark. I also want to say that I understand why you were too afraid to leave Tess, but I hope you understand why I just did what I did. It's because I want you to be safe, and even if that means you're safe with somebody else, better that than you marrying her and being unhappy forever.'

I know Tristan's friend will be back any second, so I need to go. As I leave, I tell Tristan that I only want what's best for him, but as I make my exit, he doesn't say anything in return, leaving me to wonder what might happen next and if I will ever see him again.

EPILOGUE

I t's been three months since I gate-crashed Tristan and Tess's wedding and ensured that the pair of them were separated before any legally binding vows could be made. A lot has happened since that crazy time, and it's only with the benefit of hindsight that I can look back on it all and accurately say whether or not the right things were done at the right time.

Despite not expecting Tess to be arrested so dramatically at the wedding venue when she was still in her wedding dress, her time in custody was almost as explosive as what happened at the altar. That's because Tristan told me that when it came time for him to be spoken to by the police, they informed him that Tess had continued to be an angry and aggressive presence at the station, and rather than staying quiet or denying any charges, she had openly admitted to harming her partner before saying that he deserved it and that this wasn't over yet. That was hardly the best defence she could have used, but such was her rage at being exposed so brutally in front of all of her family and friends that she seemed incapable of calming down, and things only got worse for her when Tristan gave a detailed timeline of all the abuse he had suffered at her hands, including showing the police some of his cuts and bruises.

Even with all that, convictions in cases of domestic abuse are still shockingly rare, but because the accused had no good defence for what had happened in the video, coupled with the way she behaved in custody and compounded by Tristan's testimony, Tess was sentenced to eleven months in prison.

But while that particular case was closed, another remains open, even to this day, because as of yet, the police still don't know who stabbed Mark or why. There were no witnesses to the incident at all, or at least none who are willing to come forward, and considering that doing so ourselves would be bad news for Tristan and myself, we are happy to let the case go unsolved for as long as possible. Maybe the police will never close it, but that's okay, as long as they never know what really happened. And the more time that passes, the more it seems that will be the case.

There's something else that the passage of time will help too.

My and Tristan's relationship.

Despite there being a need for the dust to settle on what happened on his wedding day, Tristan insinuated that there could be something between us in the future after I had expressed my love for him. I knew I would have to bide my time there, and that is what I did, but over the last few months, the pair of us have started to see each other with increasing regularity.

We're keeping it under wraps for now to be sensible, not telling anyone that we are romantically involved with anybody else, but Tristan has been to my house several times, and I've been to his too, and a lot has happened on those occasions. We've talked in depth about all the things we went through with our previous partners and how it has affected our trust issues going forward. We have shared several deep and passionate kisses when it became clear that our mutual attraction was only growing stronger in the presence of each other. And we have even ended up in bed together a couple of times, the pair of us giving in to our desires and sharing wonderful nights together in which we lay in each other's arms and watched as the sun came up on the other side of the curtains.

I have no doubt now that Tristan and I will be together officially one day, but there's no rush. As Tristan said to me the last time we were in bed, we've waited this long in our lives to find each other and fall in love, and things have worked out okay so far. We can just take things slowly and see how they develop, and that sounds good to me. But I'd be lying if I said I hadn't spent a little time fantasising about a potential wedding day with Tristan. But despite him saying that, I ultimately decided to return the dress, deciding that it was probably bad luck to one day wear the same dress for my wedding to Tristan as Tess had worn for hers. Best to have a fresh start and wear something new for my next big day. There's also the small matter of not having to pay £6,000 to keep the dress either.

I returned the dress with no issue. The only disappointment was that Chrissy was not in the shop when I went back with it. Apparently, it was her day off, which was a shame because I would have liked to thank her for all her help in the past, as well as let her know that when it came time for me to require a new dress one day, she was the person I would come to see about it. But never mind, I guess I'll see her again soon.

Maybe sooner than I think.

I have no idea who is going to be outside as I make my way to answer the knock on my front door. It's a random Saturday morning, and I'm home alone, although Tristan is due to come around later this afternoon. But this is too early for him, so if I have to guess, I'd say whoever is knocking is a delivery man dropping off a parcel for me. With Mark no longer around, I'm much less limited with my storage space in this house, so my shoe collection has been growing by the week. But then I open the door and see that it's not some-body bringing me yet another pair of shoes I ordered online. It's Chrissy, and when she sees me, she doesn't smile.

'Hello, Kate,' she says. 'Are you alone, or is Tristan with you?'

I have no idea why she is here, nor how she could possibly know that I'm seeing Tristan because nobody knows about it yet.

Or at least they shouldn't do.

'What are you doing here?' I ask, ignoring her question about Tristan for the time being, but Chrissy only asks me again.

'Yes, I'm alone,' I admit before hoping she'll answer my question now.

'You two make quite the couple,' Chrissy muses. 'Although I understand why you might be wanting to keep your relationship discreet for the time being.'

'What are you talking about?'

'Don't be dumb, Kate. I know you're much smarter than that. You're even smart enough to fool the police, which is no small feat.'

Oh my God. How the hell does Chrissy know so much?

'I don't know what you mean?' I try, but Chrissy just shakes her head at me.

'Yes, you do. You and Tristan are smart. You've got away with something naughty, haven't you? Or at least you thought you had.'

Chrissy knows what Tristan and I did to Mark. But how?

I look behind her then, anxiously checking to see if she has brought the police with her today. But there's nobody on the street behind her, and she assures me that no one is coming.

'Relax. I've not told anybody what I know,' she says. 'Nor do I intend to. I just want to know why you did everything that you did.'

'Everything I did?' I say, but Chrissy has no patience for me feigning ignorance, so I stop that tactic now and just ask her a simple question. 'How?'

'The first thing I thought was unusual about you was when I caught you snooping at the order book at the dress shop,' Chrissy says, her hands in her pockets and looking rather casual for a woman who must know she is no longer welcome here. 'Do you recall that day? I went into the back room to check on a dress for you, but when I glanced at the camera monitor, I noticed you checking the book. Why was that?'

I don't say anything to that, but I'm silently cursing myself for not realising there must be cameras in the shop.

'Were you looking for information on somebody?'

Chrissy asks me, still very calm. 'Tess, perhaps. Or was it Tristan you wanted to know more about?'

I definitely say nothing to that.

'It doesn't matter, I suppose, because you ended up seeing him again anyway, didn't you?' Chrissy goes on. 'You saw him in the Carter Arms. You were there the night a body was found outside that pub, weren't you? The body of your fiancé, Mark.'

I can no longer play dumb now because my mouth is hanging open, and it's obvious I'm stunned by what Chrissy is telling me.

'How do you know that?' is all I can muster.

'Because I was there that night too,' Chrissy says. 'I go in there for a drink quite often, what with it being the nearest pub to the shop. I guess you didn't notice me sitting on the other side of the busy venue. But I noticed you. Tristan too. You looked to be having a very serious conversation in your booth. Then you left together, and I wondered where you might be going. I did consider you were having an affair, not that it was any of my business. But something much more extreme occurred then, didn't it?'

'What do you want?' I ask, wondering if this is her attempt at blackmailing me.

'I want to know why you or Tristan killed Mark,' she says. 'Because I know you were both there that night, though I suspect the police don't. Of course, I had no idea who the poor man was when I left the pub and saw all the police officers outside, taping off the scene. But when the news gave the name of his poor partner who he had been due to marry, then I knew exactly who he was. What a coincidence, hey? Mark was stabbed right outside the pub where his fiancée had just finished having a drink with another man.'

As Chrissy speaks, I'm already doing the sums in my head, trying to figure out how much money I have in my bank account to potentially pay her off with and buy her silence. Is that what this is all about? Money? Maybe so, because she knows I placed an order for a £6,000 dress, so she must think I have lots of disposable cash. The problem is, I have far less than she realises.

'Relax. I'm not going to tell anybody,' Chrissy says before I've even had a chance to ask her to name her price, though I'm not quite sure I believe that because she looks very serious. 'I am interested in finding out how and why Mark died, though, and I do hope you have a good answer for me.'

It would seem that me delivering that good answer might be the thing that stops Chrissy taking what she knows to the police, so I decide that honesty is the best policy here and tell her everything.

'He was abusing me,' I say sadly. 'He was controlling me. Tristan had the same problem with Tess. That's why we met that night in the pub. We were going to go to the police and tell them everything about our partners. But Mark ambushed us outside the pub with a knife. It was self-defence, I swear it was!'

I'm praying that Chrissy believes me and that it's a good enough answer to keep her from going to the authorities and telling them there is more to my story than they might believe.

'I see,' Chrissy says, nodding. 'That makes sense, I suppose. I heard the news about Tess Nash being sentenced for domestic violence. Who would have thought it? A woman like her doing things like that to a man like him?'

'Why are you here telling me all this?' I ask her then,

eager to know her motivation for coming to my house instead of the police station.

'I just had to know what it was all about,' Chrissy replies. 'Why you were with Tristan. Why Mark was killed. Why you were snooping at the order book in the shop. Your behaviour was very puzzling to me, Kate. Fortunately for you, I seem to be the only person who knows about it all.'

'So what do you want? Money? I don't have much.'

'I know that. You only wanted that expensive dress because Tess had ordered it, didn't you? I guess it was to impress Tristan. Well, it seems to have worked. I hope the pair of you are very happy together.'

With that, Chrissy turns away to walk back to the road, leaving me to wonder if she really did come here in peace or if there is far more to her than meets the eye, which would make her very much like me. But just before she goes, she has one more thing to say.

'If you are ever in the market for a new wedding dress, just know that I work somewhere else now. Bridal Beauty on King Street. Come and see me if you and Tristan ever get around to tying the knot. I might be able to get you a discount.'

With that, Chrissy walks away, leaving me standing on my doorstep, wondering what the hell just happened.

As I close my front door and think about how I've just dodged a very big bullet, I can scarcely believe what happened.

All this time I was so preoccupied at keeping my secrets from the man I was supposed to marry and the woman who bought that lovely dress before me.

It turns out I forgot to pay attention to the woman who sells the wedding dresses.

I guess I'll have to bear that in mind if I'm ever a bride again.

Or maybe it would be better not to tempt fate one more time.

Weddings seem to bring out another side of me - a dangerous, deadly side.

But then again, all is fair in love and war, right?

ABOUT THE AUTHOR

Did you enjoy *The Bride To Be*? Please consider leaving a review on Amazon to help other readers discover the book.

Daniel Hurst writes psychological thrillers and loves to tell tales about unusual things happening to normal people. He has written all his life, making the progression from handing scribbled stories to his parents as a boy to writing full length novels in his thirties. He lives in the North West of England and when he isn't writing, he is usually watching a game of football in a pub where his wife can't find him.

Want to connect with Daniel? Visit him at his website or on any of these social media channels.

www.danielhurstbooks.com

ALSO BY DANIEL HURST

INKUBATOR TITLES

THE BOYFRIEND
(A Psychological Thriller)

THE PASSENGER
(A Psychological Thriller)

THE PROMOTION
(A Psychological Thriller)

THE NEW FRIENDS
(A Psychological Thriller)

THE BREAK
(A Psychological Thriller)

THE ACCIDENT
(A Psychological Thriller)

THE INTRUDER
(A Psychological Thriller)

THE BRIDE TO BE
(A Psychological Thriller)

Made in the USA
Middletown, DE
23 December 2023

46721371R00168